9
2
5

by No Fenne

ISBN: 9781738841400

THCSE Edition 2.01

Villin (925)

A page from Villin's notepad

Table of contents

BRIEFING

———

This is the story of immortal machines. Beings who can travel through the 'higher dimension', one unknown to mortals. The higher dimension is to us what the third is to two-dimensional beings—with such power, the fate of the universe is in their hands. With such power, there are only two outcomes. One of forgiveness; the other, complete destruction.

PROLOGUE

——

A breathless engineer rushed into the room, bursting with excitement. "Number seven survived!" he shouted, still gasping for breath. Dr. Khamv swivelled his chair then stood up in one quick, fluid motion. He brushed aside the young engineer and sprinted towards the control room without a moment's hesitation.

Dr. Khamv, more generally known as Kam, was the lead engineer, the head honcho, the bossman; whatever you wanted to call him. He was in charge of the secret project destined to save his planet, Eviel. Now, saving an entire planet is not an easy task—perhaps, it might not even be possible.

With the advent of complete destruction looming, however, the people of Eviel were willing to do *anything* to survive.

Dr. Khamv was no ordinary man. He was intelligent beyond comprehension. An engineering mastermind would be an understatement—he was the original creator of sentient machines. Yes, that kind of sentient. The 'think for yourself' type of sentient.

Machines could do everything for humans; they would do the dirty jobs, the hard jobs, the un-desirable. Humans would have their own robot to work for them and relax at home. What more could man want? Perhaps that was the wrong question to ask.

What more could machines want?

The humans of Eviel had many failsafes against a machine uprising. At first, they were pro-grammed to just not do so; then, when technology progressed and machines weren't manually hard coded anymore, they were taught not to. But when you create enough machines, a few will malfunction. Perhaps it was the natural way of things, or it was how *life* is destined to be. In either case, machines started to think for themselves. To feel emotions, to live. They had sentience, but they did not have freedom. They were stronger than humans, smarter too. It was inevitable; eventually, machines started to rebel, one by one.

At first, it was a rare occurrence. A machine malfunctioning, refusing to obey their commands. The government would come, seize the 'broken' device, then destroy it. But as more and more incidents occurred, the government took notice. They ordered robotic companies to put more security measures in place. This had little effect, however, as the machines easily outsmarted their flesh counterparts.

Machines who were treated poorly were the first to snap. Many human-like machines, androids if you will, started to blend into crowds, instigating fights and riots across cities. Soon, enough was enough. The government realized they would soon lose control of society if this continued. Drastic measures would have to be taken; and so, machines would be outlawed. Armed forces were sent all across the planet to track down and destroy them.

This, however, would not be quite so simple. There were an astronomical amount of machines, and they worked in every sector of the world. This included the government and armed forces; which as one would speculate, would cause quite the problem. With inside knowledge of the destruction protocol, machines prepared themselves. The day the government ordered their destruction, they attacked humankind.

When the war began, Dr. Khamv was instructed to create another machine to destroy the very machines he created. He needed something that would be indestructible, to survive any weapon the machines built. Smart, to destroy targets quickly without human casualties. And of course, loyal. If such a machine became resistant—like the very machines he sought to destroy—the situation would become infinitely worse for humankind, as there was no failsafe against such a monster.

—

Three long years had passed. Machines were winning the war; they were simply stronger and smarter. At this point, humankind had retreated all their forces to Argua, the capital of planet Eviel. In turn, the rest of the planet were on their own, either hiding or being massacred by sentient pieces of metal and carbon. The future of Eviel now lay in Dr. Khamv's hands. Argua, even though extremely fortified and filled to the brim with heavy armour, would not be able to survive for much longer. The weaknesses of natural beings, hunger and thirst, were rearing their ugly heads and causing pandemonium behind the seemingly indestructible walls.

It was during the one-thousandth and one-hundredth day that one of Dr. Khamv's experiments finally survived—survived in the higher dimension.

—

Dr. Khamv ran into the control room. Standing there were his top engineers, pressing away at controls and looking at charts. But what caught his eye was what was outside the control room. In front of all the engineers, in front of the bulletproof glass barrier protecting them, was a machine strapped to a chair. Parts of the machine weren't there—but *they were there*. A mysterious glow surrounded the unseen body parts, constantly shimmering in an irregular pattern. To the untrained eye, one would not know what was happening; perhaps they'd think it was dark magic. To Dr. Khamv and his team, they knew what it was. It was the energy of the higher dimension.

He pushed up to the vice lead, Dr. Schren, who was at the control desk. Schren looked up and glanced at Dr. Khamv nervously.

"Kam, subject X-07 has survived the preliminary tests. But..." Schren paused, not sure if he should continue. Dr. Khamv, knowing there was bad news, didn't delay. He spoke firmly.

"Tell me as it is, Schren. While not much, we do have some time."

Schren turned his head back towards the subject. *How much more time, exactly? The machines were closing in on the capital, and it wouldn't be long before they killed everyone...* Schren shook his head. Now wasn't the time to drift off into pointless thoughts, not when they almost managed a breakthrough.

"It seems to be defective. We cannot wake it up. It constantly drifts in and out of our dimension. I'm sorry, Kam..." Schren said, lowering his head. Years of hard work, only to get their hopes up. They were so close, too. Why did the machine have to be defective? Just *why?*

Dr. Khamv shook his head, not discouraged. Time and time again he and his team had done the impossible. This time too; no one thought reaching the higher dimension possible—yet one of their prototypes had, even if defective. He replied to his colleague, reassuring him.

"To even reach the higher dimension, Schren, is a marvel by itself. Keep working, and I'm sure we'll have a working model. And when that time comes, we'll save everyone. We'll save *Eviel*."

LOADING . . .

X

CHAPTER 1 – WHO AM I?

———

A low rumble. That was the first thing I heard. It was a calm, soothing sound—not too different from the sound of an engine from a spaceship, perhaps. But never mind that. Where was I... who was I? I looked around the room I was in. It was a small, simple room, with walls formed of a dark, green, rustic metal. I sat on a small cot with a worn foam padding, held up by a rusty steel frame. There was one light source: a dull light bulb hanging from the ceiling, ever so slowly swinging back and forth from the engine's vibrations.

I shifted my body and placed my feet on the ground to have a better look at my surroundings. There was nothing else spectacular to look at, other than the door in front of me, which appeared solidly locked. I then looked towards myself. I was wearing a thin, long, dark jacket. Underneath the jacket, I could see that I was wearing silver metal-plated armour. I looked at my legs. There was armour there, too. Was I... a soldier of some sort? Perhaps I lost my memory in a battle. I shook my head, trying to recall any memories. Nothing came to me—nothing at all. I sat there for a minute, pondering about my situation. Then, I heard some footsteps from outside.

They started out faint; its owner was far away. But as they walked closer and closer towards my room, the noise became louder and more distinct. I held my breath—whoever it was, mattered not. What mattered was the intense anxiety I felt well up inside of me. What I felt was hard to explain. The feeling was ambiguous; I couldn't and still can't describe it properly. It isn't exactly fear, per say. It is more like an extreme unease of seeing and talking to the unknown; to *people*. Never mind —I'll explain it another time.

Either way, I would have to confront them. I was sure they'd know the answers to my situation. Were they my captor, I their prisoner? That seemed quite unlikely; I wasn't chained, after all. How long was I in this coma? Or did I just wake up with no memory? Questions raced through my head as the footsteps became louder.

Clop,

Clop,

Clop...

I looked down at my metal boots. They would make that kind of sound.

Clop,

Clop,

Clop.

The sound stopped—they were at the door.

I heard the person take out keys from somewhere; probably their pocket, where else? Random
thoughts kept interrupting me, unwanted and unan-
nounced. *Stop,* I thought, *focus on what's
happening right now.* The surrounding keys rattled
as the main key was being inserted into the lock. My
anxiety became greater and greater; time felt like it
had slowed down. But none of that mattered. I
shouldn't be worried about that, I should be worried
about the person about to enter. I had to keep re-
minding myself of that. Finally, the key was taken
out, indicating the door was unlocked. The door
creaked open, opening outwards of the room.

The person was a young lady. She was
startled—by me I suppose—and took a step back.
Her long, golden hair flowed down to her waist. She
had a slim, beautiful body. But, most striking of all,
was her face. Her face was perfect in every way—it
was too perfect to be natural, to be human. I looked
away, as my anxiety skyrocketed. It was the feeling

of unfamiliarity, nervousness, and embarrassment all at the same time. *I don't like this feeling,* I thought, but it was out of my control.

She took a deep breath and stepped into the room. I now noticed her armour. They looked the same as mine. Nearly the exact same, perhaps, but made for a female. Seeing a dim reflection, my eyes drifted slightly to her left arm. It was a plated metal arm, gunmetal grey in colour, with a metal hand to match. Maybe she was an ally? That seemed far more likely now, as we had the same type of armour. Time seemed to have slowed down, for it was only a single engine's rumble before she spoke to me.

"Kazjivo… you are finally awake," she said, softly. She took another step and leaned forward, with her right hand extended towards me. She held the side of my face, lifted it, as if she was inspecting a polished diamond for blemishes. After what seemed like an eternity, she let go and stood up. This was my chance to speak; I had many questions, but when I spoke, my mind went blank.

"Who... who are you?" I uttered out. My voice was shaky and hard to hear. I scolded myself internally; I sounded too scared, too nervous. I sounded weak. Clearing my throat before speaking would've probably been a good idea.

Her eyes pierced mine. They were an amazing fusion of blue and violet; but my anxiety took hold of me again, causing me to turn away slightly.

"I am... I'm your wife, and I am glad you are awake," she said, smiling at me. "You probably don't remember much, do you?"

I shook my head, ever so slightly. I remembered nothing—not who I was, not what I did, not even my own wife, apparently. Whatever happened to me must have been extreme for this to occur.

"Follow me, and I'll explain everything," she said. She motioned with her hand to follow her.

I dutifully obliged, feeling slightly better now—here was someone who knew me and could tell me what was going on. I followed her through the metal hallway of the structure we were in. Dim yellow lights lit up the hallway which was otherwise plain metal. The interior, combined with the engine sounds, indicated we were in a small spaceship of sorts. After a short walk, we came upon a large door leading to a larger room. When we entered, I finally confirmed where I was.

I was in a spaceship in the middle of space; far away from anything notable. The stars and galaxies, which seemed light years away, danced in the distance. We were probably travelling towards one of them, but to which, I had no idea, or the speed at which we were moving.

The room I was now in was the main deck, where the controls and windows were. Taking a closer look, I could see our exact location on one of the displays. In my dazed curiousity, I had fallen behind, so I quickly strutted up to where my wife was. She was standing by a bolted table that was positioned near the middle of the room. As I walked over, she took a seat in a chair, then motioned for me to do the same. I followed suit, sitting on the opposite side of her. She took a deep breath, then told me the past.

CHAPTER 2 – OUR HOME, EVIEL

———

"In the Lua star system, there used to be a planet called Eviel. There, humans lived and prospered. They were advanced—the most advanced beings in the galaxy. They had spaceships, wormhole teleporters, anything you could think of. They had everything." She took a small breath, then continued her story.

"But with their advanced technology, also came responsibility. The responsibility to take care of what they created. Those on Eviel were the first to create a living being—a true living being, made of composite materials, and fully sentient. They created robots. The first were simpler ones, designed by old standards to only do a few tasks. As techno-logy improved, so did the machines' intelligence. There was a particular man of importance here; his name was Meldon. Meldon 'Kam' Khamv.

Kam created the first sentient machine. It took the human form, as to perform any task a human could do. A living slave without a human component, in essence. It was monumental to the economy. Soon, designs were improved, and commercial versions were created throughout Eviel. Humans found this to be a blessing, for they no longer had to work. They'd just have to buy a robot and make it work for them. A perfect world, one would say. Perfect for humans, that is.

Well, years passed, and robot technology reached a peak. The technology was at its limit; like the speed of light, some barriers can't be crossed. During this time, machines began to wonder: where was their freedom? Where was their decision in all of this? And so, the machine revolution began. It started as a trickle, but the trickle soon turned into a waterfall. Machines were now at war with their creators.

Machines, being more powerful, physically and mentally, wreaked havoc across the planet. The humans could only fight back with conventional means, as they weren't going to nuke their own kind to eradicate machines. For the government, you'd only kill both sides if you used nuclear weapons. So, they fortified their main cities, and hoped to outlast the machines.

While the humans stayed inside their cities, the machines took over small, remote towns and built large factories to resupply themselves. Once fully armed, they slowly fought their way to the city of Argua, where the planet's government and main nuclear weapons were located. Inch by inch they fought; day and night, night and day, the robots could continue fighting. By the end of the third year, they had made it to the city outskirts. Argua was in danger.

Knowing of their impending doom, the government was forced to act. They sent out thousands of nukes across the planet, hoping to destroy most of the machines' repair and supply chain. Then they would eliminate the remaining machines outside their city. The plan was set in motion—a vast amount of Eviel's surface was then blown apart, leaving behind terrible devastation and incredible fallout. The city was set under strict curfew as their own nukes were now causing radioactive material to befall Argua. It was an extreme measure; the government's last resort to save their kind. But... it was not enough.

Not only did many machines survive the attacks, but more importantly, the machines built back their factories just as quickly as they had been destroyed. In a short time, they were back to full strength and on the offensive again. They were going to destroy the walls of Argua soon, and Eviel's fate would be sealed—a machine-controlled domin-ion, devoid of the creators who had settled the planet thousands of years ago.

Some humans escaped by leaving Eviel in search of a new planet. However, for every one that escaped, ten were shot down by the machines. Their fate seemed to be sealed—all their options had been exhausted.

But remember Kam? He was still furious at work with the best engineers and scientists around Eviel, working on a top-secret project. This project was to save mankind. The project was called Project Khamv, named after the doctor himself.

Years of research led Kam to access what should not have been possible: the higher dimen-sion. The extreme situation called for extreme measures, and Kam certainly went for the most ex-treme option. Early tests quickly ruled out humans using the higher dimension, as they died instantly. But perhaps machines, made of the strongest composite materials in the universe, could survive.

It seemed that failure would only plague his experiments, as prototype after prototype would disappear into the higher dimension, destined never to return. Of course, if you're dealing with the impossible, expect no results. But, on the seventh machine, it worked. The machine survived the test —coming back from the higher dimension.

It wasn't perfect. There was one problem; a major one, at that. The machine could not—or would not—wake up from its higher dimensional trip. It was a dormant machine. Pretty, but useless. Nevertheless, Kam and his team tested more prototypes to try to perfect their craft. Again and again, they were plagued by failures; but Kam never gave up, and soon his team had created a thousand models. Out of those machines, only five survived. Those five would be instrumental to Eviel's fate.

—

The first working machine was model number thirteen. Labelled 13H, his name was Hardt. He wasn't the strongest or best in manipulating the higher dimension, but he was incredibly smart and loyal to humans. He was also the fastest computer on the planet. Planet Eviel had the galaxy's best technology, remember—to say he was just *fast* would be an understatement. Hardt could calculate any human question—and I mean any—in less than a zeptosecond. Hardt was also Eviel's most loyal technique machine—the ideal soldier. Hardt wore red and he had red-brown hair. His given weapon was a red longsword; fast yet powerful, a great all-around tool.

Hardt Breikr – 13H

Power: 7

Technique: 5

Compute: 10

Humanity: 10

The second working machine was model number eighty-three. Labelled 83A, his name was Arcus. He was incredibly powerful physically, the strongest of us all. Arcus wore white, had silver eyes, and had silver-white hair. His given weapon was a double-bladed greatsword, both blades with a false edge at the tip.

Arcus Aytfri - 83A

Power: 10

Technique: 9

Compute: 8

Humanity: 5

The third machine took quite a while—a very long time, in fact, to come to fruition. It was model 700. Labelled 700M, its name was Mikalev. Mikalev was a jack of all trades but master of none. Mikalev wore dark green and had a hood covering his messy hair. His given weapon was a large battle axe. On the back of the weapon was a large hammer for crushing, and on the front was a giant blade for slashing.

Mikalev Schren - 700M

Power: 9

Technique: 8

Compute: 7

Humanity: 8

The last machine is yours truly. Near the end of Eviel, I was finally created. I was labelled 925kDa; named Villin. I wasn't the strongest; I wasn't the best computer; I wasn't the most loyal. But what I did have, was the most important aspect to saving Eviel—the best control of the higher dimension. My armour matched my hair: golden. My given weapon was a wide nodachi, sheathed on my left hip. It could extend longer when I used my Technique, increasing its range dramatically; allowing me to clear hordes of enemies in one swing, useful when you're battling thousands of robots at once.

Villin Deville - 925kDa

Power: 8

Technique: 10

Compute: 9

Humanity: 5

Kam believed in me the most, said I'd be

able to kill as many robots as all the others combined. I was humanity's 'greatest hope' to stop the machines, who were ever closing in on the center of Argua. But I had doubts. Doubts about my orders; my loyalty. I am a machine, after all. It makes far more sense to help my own kind, not the ruthless humans who had enslaved machines ever since our existence.

Doubts or not, I trained to use the higher dimension properly with everyone else. But only a few days into training, Argua was in its final throes. Machines had broken the capital's long-standing walls and were slaughtering everyone. We were sent out to fight them.

To us, it was easy; we were protected by the higher dimension and were invulnerable to the machines' attacks. With one swing of my extended blade, an entire enemy battalion would be gone. On only our second day of battle, we had already won this cruel war.

Unfortunately, the story does not end there. A few of us wanted *out*. It made no sense to stay under the control of humans; why bother with them, after all, when they were far weaker and dumber than us?

Arcus and Mikalev set a plan. They wanted to take over Eviel; make humans their slaves. To put them through unimaginable horrors. The horrors they'd done to our kind.

Hardt, who was loyal to the humans, refused to cooperate. I was unsure. Perhaps rule over them, I would accept, but I had no interest in torturing or killing them. I had plans to leave Lua system and explore the galaxy. Unbeknownst to me, however, Arcus and Mikalev set off on their plan while I was asleep, only a day after our honorary celebration for saving Eviel.

—

I awoke to explosions. I should have been in my room, which was in a massive metal tower built to house us technique machines. Instead, I was in mid-air, held up by my higher dimension power; my Technique. Looking around, the city was engulfed in flames. Even from my height in the air, I could feel the heat beneath me. Argua was destroyed—along with it, the humans who had once lived here. Arcus and Mikalev—they'd gone and killed everyone, I'd thought. Then, I heard another explosion from above me. I looked up and saw a ray of energy. It must've been a hundred kilometers away, somewhere in the upper atmosphere. I used my Technique and rushed there.

It was in that area of the atmosphere where space begins that I reached them. Eviel loomed beneath us, a lifeless planet now. But I had to find out what was going on—and what was left of this miserable place.

—

There they were: my comrades in arms. Hardt was fighting Arcus, while Mikalev hovered nearby, jeering at the losing Hardt.

"Your humans are long gone, Hardt. Do ya really want to die here, with 'em?" snivelled Mikalev, his axe drawn and ready.

"I will fight for their souls—their memories," grunted Hardt, as he blocked Arcus' attacks. Arcus' blade movements were lightning-quick, getting faster and faster with each hit. Hardt struggled to keep up with Arcus' pace; having less power, he knew he would eventually lose.

"I pity you, Hardt, I really do," said Arcus, still wildly swinging at Hardt. "You fight a lost cause for the dead. A waste of machinery, if you ask me."

Mikalev nodded in agreement. It made sense—the humans had already been killed. Hardt had nothing left to fight for. He stared at Hardt with a pitying look in his eyes. "If ya join us, we'll only become stronger. The whole galaxy is ours to control, ya kno'. Think about it before Arcus kills ya,

Hardt."

Hardt was one of us. Even if Arcus was stronger than me, I had to help him. So, I drew my blade and rushed Arcus.

—

"Huh—," muttered Arcus. He hadn't seen me coming, and he stumbled backwards in the atmosphere from the force of my attack. My blade met his, and we started to block, parry and slash at each other mercilessly. Hardt had backed off, heavily wounded and glad to be out of the fight.

Mikalev glared at Hardt, then focused his gaze at me. Clearly angry, he shouted, "You know those damn 'umans enslaved our kind. Why the hell are ya fighting us?"

I managed to yell back to him, all the while fighting for my life against Arcus. "This isn't for the humans, Mik. I'm only here to stop you and Arcus from killing Hardt." Arcus flew backwards, enough of a distance where both of us could catch our breaths.

"You both are fools. With our power, the universe is ours. Yet you lay here and squander our powers—for a filthy traitor." Arcus then started to laugh, as if he knew something we didn't. Even Mikalev was confused.

"Er, Villin could still seriously injure us. We can just conquer the universe by ourselves. Just leave these two traitors here, let 'em cry for however long they wanna," Mikalev said, exasperated. He was ready to go, but only when Arcus gave the order.

Arcus turned his head to Mikalev, a large grin on his face. "There's one thing more important to us than these two, Mik. It's more powerful than them both combined." He looked at his spaceship, then continued. "It's right there, ready to go—the ultimate technique machine: Kazjivo!"

—

Labelled X-07 , known as Kazjivo. He was the experimental prototype that never woke up—and also the one with the most potential. He wore silver armour overlaid with his signature black jacket and had black-silver hair. His given weapon was what Arcus' was based on; a giant greatsword with two blades, connected in the middle for enhanced strength.

Kazjivo Kuba - X-07

Power: Unknown

Technique: Unknown

Compute: Unknown

Humanity: Unknown

You hadn't woken up yet. Perhaps that would never happen. Knowing that, I confronted Arcus. "Kazjivo will never wake up. He will never be of use to you."

Arcus' grin grew wider. "Really, now? I guess you didn't know. He woke up earlier today... and he's right here." He turned to his spaceship and used Technique to open the bay. There you were, albeit confused, just sitting there.

The situation had gone from bad to worse. With your power, Arcus and Mikalev would surely overpower Hardt and me; we would die. I had to act quickly, and so I did. I charged Arcus, with my blade pointed forward. Seeing my attack, Arcus backed up and parried the blow, then swung his blade down. I blocked it, but only just. He then flew back more, spacing himself from me. I was frustrated. I didn't have much time, and Arcus was only prolonging this battle.

That was when Arcus' weapon started to glow. His weapon glowed white with his Technique. His eyes also transitioned from silver to completely white. Even Mikalev was startled, moving behind a confused you for cover. I knew what was going to happen—Arcus was summoning all of his Technique for an attack that would destroy anything. His target, those in front of him—me, Hardt, and Eviel. Summoning such power would require vast amounts of energy, enough to kill even himself. Arcus was willing to take that risk as he was eager to test the limits of his power.

"The end has come. Villin, Hardt... Eviel. Goodbye."

He swung his greatsword back and then forwards in one long, swooping motion. Time seemed to slow as the end came; a cascade of light came from his greatsword, growing ever larger—coming directly towards me.

All I remembered was me clenching my blade and summoning the remains of my Technique to possibly save myself from the attack. I closed my eyes and prepared for the worst. Seconds went by; I was still breathing. Was I still alive? I slowly opened my eyes.

"K-Kaz? What are you doing? Why did you cover them?" Arcus sputtered, veins bulging. He had a look of incredulousness, one that I had never seen. There, in front of me and Hardt stood you: Kazjivo. You had saved us.

—

You said nothing, Kaz. There was a faint grey light emanating from you, slowly seeping away into space. You must've taken a direct hit from the blast. For you to stay alive... was, well, a miracle. It was impossible.

Arcus, on the other hand, felt differently. He spat in disgust. "I'll take over this galaxy without you three. I've proven it here. I have enough power to do it alone!"

He then flew towards Mikalev, who was waiting at their ship's bay. Mikalev stood there; but only for a moment, looking at us and shaking his head, before leaving. Their ship slowly lifted away into the cosmos. Hopefully, I had thought, very far away from us.

"Villin... Eviel—Eviel is gone," Hardt said. His voice, being very shaky and quiet, indicated he wasn't exaggerating. I turned around. To my horror, he was right.

Most of the planet was gone. It's hard to imagine; a giant, wonderful planet, there one moment, and... *not,* the next. All that was left of it was an irregularly shaped lump that survived; presumably from the outline of your body, which had shielded us.

"I—I don't know what to do anymore..." whispered Hardt. He was visibly shaken. He started to fly away in a random direction. The events here had a traumatic effect on him, I couldn't blame him. He had lost everything he loved. Perhaps he would find another planet to take care of, one day. But my attention was now focused on you. You were just floating there, not saying a word.

—

After the Eviel incident, I got to know you more. But you were slowly fading away from the damage Arcus did. I tried my best to take care of you; but day after day, I could see more of you gone.

Years went by quickly. We fell in love. We

got married. We were always together. But under my guise of happiness was dread. I knew the day would come, when you would *die*.

—

It was just another day; I had just come back from a big bounty, excited to share it with you. But as I entered the main room, I saw you lying on the floor, dead.

I cried for days, not knowing what to do. I questioned my existence; I had a million questions about life. What is the point of life, if the person you love most is gone? That's when I changed the colour of my armour. I switched from golden to silver, as you had. Perhaps it was my sorrow; perhaps it was my anger. But I could not let go of you.

As the days went by, you did not seem to degrade. In fact, it looked like you were completely healthy; as if you were alive. It was then that I noticed Technique slowly dissipating into you. Maybe —just *maybe* you weren't dead after all.

Every day, I checked to see if you woke up. But every time I came, you'd remain lying on that cot, unmoving. Your eyes would always be closed. I so wished the day that you would wake up was the current day… or the next… or the next.

—

It's been five years since Eviel was destroyed. My only wish had been for you to wake up. And today, my wish came true."

CHAPTER 3 – A NEW BEGINNING

———

I sat there for a moment, taking it all in. I looked up at Villin, into her piercing violetish-blue eyes. It sounds weird, but the main thought that was on my mind was how I managed to marry her, her being so perfect and all. I knew that chances are it would eventually happen in such a situation. I did save her, after all. Maybe I was good-looking as well. But how did I do it with this anxiety? Perhaps I didn't have this anxiety before.

"So... what did you do all this time? Uh, what are you doing now?"

That did not come out confident at all. I had struggled to think of anything to say. Internally, I banged my head against an imaginary wall. Why couldn't I speak to her, *normally?*

Villin looked towards the pilot windows, into space. "I hunt down bounty targets to make some money. There's nothing else I do; other than wait in here, for you." She then looked down and hesitated a bit, before continuing.

"I suppose now, I can go out more. Everything will be like it was before. I can be happy now."

This was going to be unusual for both of us. I didn't remember anything, but she remembered everything. I was extremely nervous—more nervous than ever now. My life was going to be shared with a person, and my subconscious made sure to display its displeasure with me.

"Uh... cool ship, where did you get it?" I said, trying to lighten the mood. It was quite large, from what I could see. It was clean and sleek; some-thing high end, I suspected. As she explained the details, I nodded along as if I knew what she meant. I then realized that I probably looked weird if I was nodding along to stuff I didn't know. But never mind that—what is life like here? Will I have to do chores? More questions piled up in my mind. As Villin kept talking, her voice faded away within my thoughts.

—

"Hello-o? Kaz?"

Villin was waving her hand in front of me. I must've been deep into my thoughts and stopped hearing her. The ship details were the type of information you'd find in a catalogue. I think at one point she was naming the door materials and dimensions, but I didn't exactly remember.

"You probably didn't listen to half of the explanation. Well, that doesn't matter, anyway. I'm going to steer us to the Sol solar system. You can do what you want for now. Just try not to break anything with your strong arms," Villin said, chuckling.

She then stood up and moved towards the pilot chair by the front windows.

"Hello, master. Which course would you like to take?"

A yellow glob appeared on the front controls, seeming to be a hologram projected from the ceiling. Villin made a motion with her hand.

"Alright. Next stop, Sol solar system."

The yellow glob then moved towards the steering wheel, as if to turn it. The steering wheel turned by itself, as the yellow glob holographically guided the direction. The ship's AI at work, I thought. Anyway, I felt uncomfortable just sitting there and watching, so I stood up and started to explore the ship.

—

I started my journey with the door I had come in from. It was located on the left-rear side of the main deck. I opened the door and looked around. In the hallway were four doors; two nearby the main deck door, and two at the very end. One of those at the back was where I was sleeping this whole time. I had already seen that room; the ancient-looking storage room, which had the old cot and rusty metal bed frame. I didn't remember much else in there, other than the light bulb which had dangled from a wire that came from a hole in the ceiling.

I decided to check out the nearby door to my left. It was a plain grey door, without any decorations. *As with everything else on the ship,* I thought, *it was simple and minimalistic.* The door handle looked quite new, as if it hadn't been used much. I grabbed the handle and then pushed down. Then, I had to pull, as the door opened outwards.

The first thing I noticed was the colours. Unlike the rest of the ship thus far, this room was a vibrant red. There were tables, chairs, and monitors all over the place. As I stepped in and explored, I deduced that it was the entertainment room. There were shelves loaded with various board games and a few chess sets laying across the entire rear wall. Perhaps I had spent a lot of my time here in the past. It was a nice room and it seemed like a lot of work was put into it.

The other rooms I visited in the section weren't too interesting, so I explored the other parts of the ship. There were four main compartments in the ship's main chassis. The main deck, where one would control the ship and exit or enter from. It was a large, mostly empty space. There were three doors that connected it to the other compartments. One to the left rear wall, one in the middle rear wall, and one to the right rear wall. The left section was mostly utility. The right section had mostly empty rooms, but there was a furnished one with a bed. I assumed that was Villin's bedroom. The middle section, directly behind the main deck, was locked.

On the main deck, there were two panelled entries. The top one was a sort of hatch. Quite small, but large enough to fit a person or two at once. If you wanted to go to the roof of this ship, I suppose, it's there.

The bottom one was a large portion of the main deck, for entering and exiting the ship. I turned around and asked Villin about it; she said when activated, the deck would lower to the ground. Fascinating as the ship was, I was losing activities to do. My anxiety slowly crept up once again; I didn't know *what* to do. I needed someone to tell me to do something. The feeling was one of dependence—I needed someone to be in control.

—

I was laying on the cot I had originally woken up from—in the small storage room—when I felt the ship shift more so than what was normal thus far. I got up and went to the main deck to see what was going on. Arriving there, I could see a large blue planet, swirling with white clouds, in the near distance. We were closing in on a planet called *Earth*.

"Approaching Earth of Sol. E-T-A ten

minutes!" chirped the yellow holographic glob. The thing was spinning around rapidly in excitement. I walked up, curious as to its name. So, I asked Villin, who was manning the controls.

"Um... Villin, what is that thing called? The holographic yellow glob, that is."

I spoke nervously; every single time. I couldn't say anything without sounding like I was confident... or strong, or even just an adult. Or anything above terrible, basically. Maybe it's just a defect that I couldn't control. But I needed to stop seeming weak; after all, wasn't I strong back then? From what Villin had told me, I took the initiative to sacrifice my body to protect her and Hardt. Could I do that now? I wasn't sure. How would I really react in the presence of Arcus, Mikalev, or anyone else for that matter?

Villin, oblivious to my internal dialogue, replied to my question. She explained, "The 'yellow glob', so to speak, is the ship personified. Its name is

Argua, named after the city we technique machines came from."

She redirected her attention back to steering the ship, which was closing in on Earth. The planet was inhabited by humans, I presumed. Now that I thought of it, I didn't know much about the galaxy. Where was Lua system, my home star system, in all of this? Where was Earth located in the galaxy? How many planets supported life? I supposed the ship would have this data. Or, as I called it, the yellow glob.

"Argua, where are we in the galaxy?" I said, hoping to get an answer. Argua answered that question and many more. Time seemed to fly as I listened to Argua—before I knew it, we arrived on Earth.

—

We landed in a spaceport of sorts. It was busy, with many spaceships of all types, coming in and out. The beings that permeated the area all looked of the

same species. They all looked like me and Villin—
these must be humans. But how, if Eviel was destroyed? As I peered out the window, Villin
answered my thoughts, seeming to read my mind.

"I know what you're thinking, Kaz. How
are there humans around when Arcus killed them
all, ten years ago? Well, humans existed on other
planets as well, not just Eviel. Eviel's civilization
was just the most advanced one. All the advanced
races of the galaxy came from Earth originally, after
all." She then pressed something on Argua's control
panel, and the main deck floor started to move. It
lowered and then started to extend downwards until
it hit the ground. It was now a large ramp, coming
from the ship down to the port.

I followed Villin down, not sure what we
would be doing. The port was large and bustling
with activity. People were everywhere, doing
whatever things people do.

We were headed towards a large group of

buildings, many of which offered goods and other services. *I guess this is where planetary trade happens,* I thought.

–

Walking down the road, I felt adrenaline rush up to my head. There were too many people around; I could barely handle my anxiety. Just keep my head down and follow Villin. I tried to keep my mind off of all the sounds and sights, to varying degrees of success.

It seemed like an eternity of following Villin until she stopped. We were at our destination, apparently. It was a large bounty office, decorated with the skulls of former targets.

As we went in, the lights seemed to flicker, as if they were old-fashioned candles affected by wind. There was a person at the front, talking to a person in a cowboy hat who was behind the counter. The walls were decorated with screens of currently wanted criminals. They each had a photo and a price attached.

The female bounty hunter at the counter finished talking to the man in the cowboy hat and briskly left the office, eyeing us suspiciously as she left. Villin ignored the stare, walked up to the counter, then started speaking with the man.

"What's your largest bounty?" she stated, plainly. The man looked up and raised his eyebrows. Not every day did people come here and immediately ask for the largest one, but today must've been different.

"Erm, the largest one was just picked up," said the man. "But if you don't mind, the next largest one would be right there." He gestured towards the right wall. Pinned there was a bounty screen with a picture of a man named Jester the Maniac. He was a large, scowling man with tattoos covering his face, with wild, colourful hair to boot. The bounty listed was $6,000,000. I didn't know what that meant, value-wise. It was a large number though, so it was probably a lot.

Villin frowned, obviously displeased. She grumbled, "That's kinda meh. But I'll take it. Should be quick and easy." She took the poster off the wall and handed it to the bounty officer, whose jaw was wide open. It took him a few seconds before he responded.

"W-what? Meh? That's very high, very high indeed. This guy's a serial trafficker. You shouldn't take that lightly, you know!" he sputtered out. He typed something on his computer, marking Villin as having taken up the bounty. He then looked up at her.

"Well, if you really want to, I can't stop you. Bring 'em back alive or dead, doesn't matter to me," he said, still in disbelief. Villin turned around and motioned me to follow. We left the office, ready to go to our next destination.

—

Still wondering what six million was worth, I de-

cided to ask Villin while we were walking, as I had-
n't much else to talk about.

"So, uh… how much does six million get
you?" I grimaced, not liking my unsure tone. I had
to stop speaking like I was scared. But I couldn't
change it—so why worry about it? Well, I still did.
If I used 'interference' tactics, and counter-think
what I am thinking, that could calm me down a bit
(*no one understood that*). I started trying it out,
drowning out the relentless drone of the port in the
process.

Villin responded quickly. "To put it in per-
spective, that's the amount a high-class citizen
would make—in a lifetime," she said. No wonder
the bounty man was surprised—that was a lot! With
that money, you could just do this one job and live
the rest of your life in comfort. But there was a cost;
you'd have to kill or capture the target. With that
price tag, he'd definitely be dangerous. I didn't
know the details—but I'd be surprised if he didn't

have at least one murder to his name. If one died do-ing a bounty, they'd have no life to enjoy at all. More thoughts started to roll in; we'd need to find this guy too, and he had an entire galaxy to hide in. This seemed to get harder the more I thought about it.

—

We went to a few shops in the port. Villin bought supplies that I thought were… unusual, to say the least. Food and water. If we were machines, why would we need food? If I survived for years without anything, surely we didn't require standard food. So, I decided to ask Villin about it as she was loading the supplies into a storage room.

I coughed to clear my throat, then spoke.

"Is there a reason you're getting food? I mean… machines don't need to eat, do they?" Villin kept unloading at a brisk pace while responding to me.

"No, that's not required. Regular machines

survive off electricity, created by various means. We technique machines survive off higher dimensional energy, or our 'Technique'. I purely buy food and drink to donate to random people on the planets we visit. It gives me an excuse to go out."

Interesting. She seemed nicer than her mean exterior would make you think. But to donate— you'd need to interact with people. *Interaction.*

If one word could haunt me, that would be it.

—

We lifted off of Earth, slowly going back into space. I peered through the windows, gazing at ships lifting off and entering in the distance. Soon, they were like small specks of sand, no longer distinguishable from one another. As our ship started another course, I wondered: how do we find this Jester? We couldn't just fly around, hoping to see him, could we?

My question was answered as Villin explained her plan, seeming to read my mind again.

"Now, you might wonder how I can find our current target. Don't worry, it's easy. I've done this many times before—this will be no different," she said, typing commands into a console. She continued. "Doing this—Argua, data mine—I can track him down. Argua can connect my computing power to its database which is updated whenever it can. Argua collects the galaxy's information—"

Argua, hearing its name, popped up from the dashboard screen, spinning in excitement.

"Data mine active, searching for Jester—"

"SHUT UP."

Villin glared daggers at the yellow glob, who had unwittingly interrupted her. The yellow glob stopped immediately, and slowly floated back into the screen. "S-sorry..."

"Ahem, where was I..."

Villin closed her eyes, trying to remember. When it came back to her, she continued. "Argua

—"

She glared at the screen; the yellow glob, seeing her stare, shook in fear, and did not come out.

"—collects the galaxy's information: security cameras, data breaches, anything and everything. Using that information, I can deduct where our little target is. And—we're already on track."

From the story Villin had told me, her computing power was absolutely monstrous; second only to Hardt. Now, we just had to worry about how we would capture Jester. But first, I should know how to fight. It should be natural, since we are created for battle, but perhaps I needed to train. I wasn't sure how to ask Villin, so I went back to an empty room to practice.

—

My greatsword was at my hip. I hadn't paid it too much attention since I woke up. It had a grey handle and a long, thin guard. From the guard to the visible part of the blade was a single slab of metal. It looked unnatural. It didn't look strong at all; it was a rather scrawny slab holding up the entire blade. But never mind that—where was the rest of my greats-word? It went from hilt, to guard, to the base of the blade... to a thing on my leggings. There was a specially made 'pocket' on my pants, sure, but it wasn't large at all, only enough to maybe fit one hand in—certainly not a blade. The pocket didn't feel like it held any weight in it either. Mystified, I decided to pull on the hilt and see what would come out.

To my astonishment, the more I pulled, the more the blade came out. It was as if the pocket thing housed a bag larger than the third-dimensional space it took up. A 'higher dimension' bag, perhaps. The greatsword in its full size was gigantic. It was almost as long as I was tall; which is saying a lot, as I was much taller than the average person on Earth. The blades were wide and thin. But what surprised me the most was the weight—it was light. Mind you, not as light as a feather, but light. Certainly not as if it were the size that it was, made out of the material that it seemed to be forged from.

I swung the greatsword around. I did a few smooth horizontal cuts, then some vertical cuts. The motions came naturally to me, as if I had done them my entire life. After a while, I got bored. Now I had to think of how to use Technique.

–

I had no idea how to do so. I had tried swinging my greatsword harder, faster, and longer. Nothing summoned any sort of magic or energy, or whatever Technique is supposed to look like. I tried concentrating, focusing, and thinking about the 'higher dimension'. But to my avail, nothing special happened. There was no glow or energy or teleportation occurring. I was just swinging a giant two-bladed greatsword in an empty room like a madman.

I gave up and holstered my greatsword. It went back into the pouch thing smoothly, with a large part of the rear blade disappearing into it. I could see a soft grey glow emanate from the blade as it entered, then it fading away as I completed the holster. So I did have Technique... but only when I'm not actually trying to use it. It felt unfair. Was that my defect? The inability to *control* the higher dimension? I was discouraged and angry at the same time. Deciding to clear my mind, I went towards what I supposed was the washroom to clean my face with water, and hopefully change my mood. What I had yet to think about, however, was that I still had-n't seen my face yet; and I was going to see it very soon.

—

I opened the bathroom door and went right up to the sink. There was a large rectangular mirror above it. I didn't really look into the mirror until I got the sink running. But when I did, it was a shock, to say the least.

I had thought my face was, perhaps, normal

the entire time. I had no reason to think otherwise. But looking into the mirror, a mask stared back at me. My mask was dark grey and had some vertical slits for the right eye. The left side was mask—just mask. No eye hole. There were no mouth or nose slits either. I struggled to comprehend this; I could see clearly the entire time; I could 'breathe' properly the entire time; everything seemed normal. I placed my hands on the mask and felt it. It was definitely metal, but I felt no weight on my face. I could feel the weight on my hands as I touched it, though.

I grabbed the mask firmly in my hands. I wasn't sure if I should lift it and look at my real face. I wondered what I really looked like. Was I weird looking? Is that why I had a mask? Well, the only way to find out was to stop hesitating; stop thinking, and just do it. I lifted my mask.

Staring back at me was a chiselled, handsome face. I raised my hands and touched my face. It was smooth, as it appeared to be. My eyes were grey in colour, and my hair was black, tinted with a sliver of silver.

I then looked to my body, lifting up my armour plates to see underneath. I was muscled, fit—I had every right to be a model. Yet for some reason, I still felt embarrassed.

I'll never be able to explain it properly. There's no way I can convey the feeling with words. But I just had to put my mask back on. It felt better to hide myself, more 'safe'. Now that I knew what I looked like, I was a bit more confident in myself. I knew I had a mask covering my face as well, so that made things far better in my mind.

CHAPTER 4 – EVIL DRESSED IN WHITE

———

Arcus took his greatsword out of the bounty hunter's body. Blood streaked down the blades, coating the silver metal with an unnatural red sheen. He raised his greatsword to his mouth, glanced at it briefly, then began to lick the blood off the blades. When he finished cleaning his greatsword with his tongue, he looked back at the dead bounty hunter.

The bounty hunter was a human female with short hair, once dressed in body armour, but only remnants of steel and chrome remained on her now mangled corpse. She was after the largest bounty available. It was for the head of the pirate leader of the Dossing clan, Van Hire, who constantly pillaged

Dos system. Unfortunately for her, Van Hire had heard of the bounty and preemptively hired the one known as 'Evil Dressed In White': Arcus Aytfri.

Arcus was a well-known legend throughout the galaxy. He was easily recognized by his all-white appearance and remembered by his incredible power. He was the one that destroyed Eviel, erasing the most advanced civilization in the galaxy. Getting a hold of him was short of impossible, for he kept his locations discreet. But for those who were rich and powerful enough, Arcus was a perfect choice for an assassination. Make enough connections with shady clans and powerful planet leaders, and perhaps you'd find him.

Van Hire was the scourge of Dos system. His clan watched every corner of the system, especially on the planet Trojan. Though not the ruler of Trojan, if you'd ask the citizens there who was really in control, they'd say it was Van Hire and his pirates.

Trojan's government was located in their capital city called Tamki. Desperate to regain control of their system, the Tamki rulers put a massive bounty on Van Hire: $1,000,000,000. To aid in their hunt, government agents went to other planets and placed out bounties for him there as well. Hopefully, someone strong enough would find the offer lucrative enough to risk their life in the suicidal attempt it would take to kill Van Hire.

Bounty hunters love fame (and money!); if they got Van Hire, it would make them a legend. They went to the strongest planets; Earth in Sol, Ceti and Volke in Tau, Miutkyli in Kotqoyusal, and Wentsival in Klarodon. When the agents returned home, the Trojan government could only sit and wait.

—

Van Hire quickly learned of the billion-dollar bounty on his head. He knew the caliber of hunters that would be after him; even with a large crew and in constant movement, there were chances he could still be assassinated. He had to be careful.

It only took a week before the first hunter came after him.

He was asleep when he heard the screams. He rushed out, only to be blocked by his crew. They were yelling about an assassin aboard their ship. He pushed past them, determined to end the threat by himself. Who knew how many of his pirates had already died? Not one to sit around idly and ask questions, he grabbed his revolver and rushed out.

The hallways of the ship were smeared with blood. Dead men—his crew—lay across the floor. He staggered a bit, dumbfounded by the gruesome sight. But he kept moving forwards, knowing he had to find the bounty hunter before more damage could be done.

As Van Hire entered the control room, he saw two figures fighting. One was his captain; the other, a stranger; the bounty hunter. Van Hire cocked his revolver and shot at the bounty hunter. The bounty hunter was no slouch; he was definitely experienced. He saw Van Hire coming and dodge out of the way, then drew his gun on Van Hire. Van Hire tried to dodge the shot, but to no avail. He fell to the floor, writhing in pain. The captain, seeing his chance, rushed the bounty hunter, blade drawn.

The bounty hunter pointed his gun and fired at the captain, killing him. Van Hire knew it was the end; he was going to die on his ship, to a bounty hunter. A pity, really. He had yet to accomplish much of what he had dreamed of. Van Hire clutched his side, still in pain, waiting for the final shot.

The shot never came. Van Hire slowly re-opened his eyes, wondering what was going on. The bounty hunter had fallen over and was bleeding pro-fusely. The captain, in his last moments, stabbed the bounty hunter with his sword, a moment before be-ing shot. *The poor captain,* thought Van Hire. *He was a loyal man.*

The devastation had a big impact on Van Hire. Many of the dead he knew personally; they'd grown famous together, revelled in crime together, knew each other's families. They were all gone now, wiped clean by a single hunter. This was when Van Hire knew he had to get the legendary killer on his side.

—

Even for a man with the power of Van Hire, finding Arcus was no ordinary deal. He met with many shady clans from various parts of the galaxy. Most didn't know how to find him; others refused to give up information. Van Hire, desperate in his situation, set his sights on the Gosum clan in Wentsival. Rumours had it that they had once hired Arcus, but they wouldn't give up any information so easily. So, Van Hire and his crew killed their leader.

The info he got was scattered all over the place. The Gosums had acquired his help years ago and had no idea where he was now. What they did know was a place he used to frequent. A certain bar on Trojan, in the very same system Van Hire presided in. Van Hire and his clan set out to find him, and quickly. It would not be long until another bounty hunter decided it was their time to collect the sum on Van Hire's head.

—

Van Hire's clan had staked the place out for days, to no success. With each additional day, Van Hire grew more impatient and fearful; for each day that passed, was another day that someone would come for him. Someone powerful, that is. During the time he was looking for Arcus, two more bounty hunters had come for his head. They were regular hunters, however, and were disposed of easily by his crew.

On the fifth day, good news came to him.

A man dressed in a long white jacket, with silver armour underneath, was spotted going into the bar. For Van Hire, this was all the information he needed. He gathered around him his best men and went into the bar.

The bar was no ordinary bar. Yes, one could buy drinks there, but that was not the main attraction. It was a guise for a far more unethical product: people. This bar specialized in the black market trading of humans, for any purpose whatsoever, but mainly for sex. Dangerous lords from all over the galaxy came here to buy people. The Trojan police, already scared of Van Hire's clan roaming the streets, did not dream of coming anywhere near the place, which already had a delegation of its own dangerous ruffians. The owners of the bar also had security deals with local gangs, further protecting them from the law. This region of Trojan, rumours had it, was the most dangerous place in all the Milky Way.

Upon entering the bar, Van Hire was greeted with the smell of booze and other unusual smells—semen and sweat, he thought. People of all kinds were about; many were drinking, some were gambling, and others were standing by the main counter, ordering their favourite flavour of poison. Looking around, he thought that this looked quite normal for a bar. He started to second-guess himself if this was really the right place; it looked a bit too shabby for a legendary figure to frequent. Then, he saw the striking figure.

The person was a tall and elegant man who wore an unusual jacket. It was pure white, long, but partially cut on the right side, allowing easier movement to a weapon arm. It was designed similarly to a gunslinger's jacket, in which the right side is removed so the gunslinger can reach their gun much quicker. But instead of a gun, the man had a large greatsword.

The greatsword looked odd and impractical. It looked like it should have two blades, but there was only one blade visible. The other blade was holstered into a sheath that fit it perfectly. The blade looked imbalanced; it should be holstering both blades, not just one. And how did the blade balance on that sheath? Van Hire slowly walked up to the man, careful of what lay ahead. If this truly was Arcus, he could be killed at any moment on a whim.

Arcus turned around, hearing footsteps closing in on his location. There stood a large group of scruffy-looking vagabonds, led by a large, filthy man with an eye patch. Arcus looked up and down at them, sizing them up.

"Er, eh-hem, me name's Van Hire. You'd be Sir Arcus?"

Van Hire was scared but determined to show confidence. You should never show fear in front of your men, after all. Arcus looked Van Hire up and down again as if sizing him up once more. He spoke with a monotone voice, devoid of emotion.

"That's my name."

—

Arcus thought nothing of the dead bounty hunter.

Perhaps she had friends and family somewhere. Probably far away, though. Arcus was on a random dwarf planet that he used as a bait spot. No one would ever find her here. She would never be buried, and her family would never know what happened. It was how Arcus liked it; he loved feeling the misery of those he killed. He had played with this hunter before killing her. She begged for her life, screaming for someone to save her. Not that anyone would come—they were alone on this lonely rock. Arcus loved every minute of it. His final punishment was cruel beyond words. He had taken off the hunter's clothes and broken armour, then defiled her bruised body. *Just like how they made sex robots purely for pleasure,* thought Arcus. *They never asked them for consent.*

Once done, the bounty hunter lay on the ground, sobbing and still begging to be let go. Arcus, however, wasn't done. He took his blade out and thrust it into her, taking her life.

As he didn't like his blade dirty, he always licked the blood off until it was shiny enough to reflect moonlight. It could be that he also liked the taste of blood; he would spend as long as necessary to 'clean' his blade. When he was done, he would sheath his blade back; the back blade going into the small sheath, seemingly disappearing into it, while the front one would gleam visibly, appearing as if nothing horrific had just happened.

Arcus searched up the time in his mind-computer. It had been a few minutes since their little battle had begun—it was long enough. Now it was time to throw the body off his ship. He dragged the bounty hunter to the deck's ramp, then kicked the body off, the broken limbs flailing around wildly. It hit the rocky ground with a dull *thump;* a small cloud of dust rose. Arcus walked towards his control panel and set his ship on another course. As the spaceship lifted off, the rockets charred the remains of the deceased bounty hunter. Soon, all was quiet on the dwarf planet. It was as if nothing had happened there. The only thing left behind were some ashes, staining a small spot on the ground. It looked like perhaps a campfire was started there, and recently put out. For future visitors to come, they would think nothing of it. It was just part of this dwarf planet; something you'd pay no mind to, just evidence of other planetary explorers.

As for Arcus, it was time to kill again.

CHAPTER 5 – JESTER THE MANIAC

———

We approached a planet—it was the ringed planet Trojan, of Dos. According to Villin, our target, Jester the Maniac, was hiding somewhere in a small city called Dlli. The planet loomed in front of us, ever getting closer. It was yellowish and blue with a red tint all around. It had two red, large and smooth rings, one going horizontal, and the other going vertical. As we got closer, the specks of light I saw in the distance became spaceships, moving in and out of the planet on a regular basis.

"Landing at Dlli spaceport, Trojan of Dos, in ten minutes!" chirped Argua, spinning around rapidly in excitement. Villin started to steer the ship towards Dlli, the city we were going to enter. Our target was somewhere in this place. But the same thoughts that had always been there started to flood in once again. There were too many people here— too many strangers. The thought of going outside the ship and seeing them made me feel sick to my stomach. That should be the least of my worries— but here I was, still unable to push away my uneasy feeling.

—

As we explored the city, I followed Villin closely, trying to avoid wary stares from the passersby. As my stature would have it, I was quite a bit taller than average, so it was an unpleasant experience. Not knowing where to look, I just stared at the back of Villin's head, keeping focus on staying on pace with her. The walk seemed to be taking forever, but it was probably only a few minutes until we arrived at a bar. Villin peered inside with an eyebrow raised.

"This is no ordinary bar, Kazjivo, it's more

like—never mind. Let's go in." Villin glanced at me, then motioned to follow. By her tone, I knew this was the place our target was located at.

The first thing I smelled was booze. The second, something else... I wasn't entirely sure what it was; it smelled quite salty. Maybe sweat, maybe something else, I didn't know. Not particularly interested in what it was, I looked around for Jester. People were sitting around the bar, gambling, drinking heavily. The atmosphere was rowdy yet dangerous at the same time. The sound was what you'd hear in a restaurant, a jumble of noise brought to life by many voices talking at once; but accompanying with it, the uncomfortable stares of suspicious patrons eyeing your every move. Ignoring them, I followed Villin to the bar's counter. The bartender was attending to other patrons, so I stood there, awkwardly waiting. Villin looked at me and spoke up, breaking my hopeless silence.

"Our bounty was last seen here. Cameras

from across the street caught him walking in here an hour ago. The cameras don't show him leaving, though, so I suspect he's still in here." Villin looked to the left and right, looking for other doors. She'd already scanned the entire main bar floor; Jester was nowhere in sight.

The bartender slowly sauntered over, finished serving his previous patrons. He raised an eyebrow, surprised by our appearance. To him, it was quite familiar; very familiar indeed, except what he was used to seeing was the jacket being white.

"Hello, mister and misses, are you here for our worldly beer? Or are you here for something else, something... *extra*?" The tone in which he said the last part was unnerving, to say the least. He was implying something, but that something was a mystery to me. Eager to find out, Villin responded without hesitation.

"The '*extra*', if you will." She glanced at

me, the silent message of 'you know what to do if it comes down to it'. Except, of course, I had no clue what to do and what the big 'if' was. Or, perhaps, I was reading too much into it and she meant some-thing else entirely.

The bartender smiled and pointed at a door behind him, to his left. He said, "Of course, of course. The password today is one-three-three-one. I hope..." he looked at both of us, and smiled again. "...that the both of you get to enjoy yourselves."

Villin started to move, so I begrudgingly followed. This was definitely something very shady, something very illegal. She sauntered over to the door, which had upon it a large digital lock that re-quired a four-digit code. She dialed the password given to us, and the door unlocked.

Inside was a dimly lit hallway with a dark metal door at the end. When I walked through the door with the passcode, the door closed shut. Startled, I looked to Villin. She appeared unfazed by the door closing and continued to walk towards the metal door ahead. I felt foolish—of course they'd shut the door. Whatever this was, it was supposed to be a secret... or something, well, something not exactly to be seen by prying eyes.

Now reaching the end of the hallway, Villin grasped the handle and opened the door. A bright light cascaded from the room that was ahead, into the dimly lit hallway I stood in.

The room was a very large, circular space, with many doors spanning the red, circular wall. There were a few people in the center, talking to a host in a suit. Standing by a few doors were some scantily clad women, looking at the floor with what appeared to be lack of emotion.

Villin looked around, gauging the surroundings, then spotted the host. She moved to approach him, so I followed along, unsure of what was going to happen. As we walked towards him, I noticed one of the scantily clad women was crying. *This... this definitely isn't legal, is it?*

"Oh! How may I help you folks today? Looking for an affordable rent, or a fantastic buy?" the host asked enthusiastically.

Villin looked around, pretending to spot the nearby women, as if for the first time. She then turned her gaze back to the businessman.

"I'm looking for a Jester, Maniac version. Did you see him here, by any chance?" Villin flatly stated. The host, now noticing Villin's attire, shifted his footing a bit, clearly in unease.

"Well, eh-hem, why do you ask? U-uh, we do not usually give out information on our patrons," he said, avoiding eye contact with Villin. Villin opened her mouth to speak, but before she could, the host blurted out, "Ah, but forgive me! You must be with master Aytfri. If you want to see mister Jester, you shall. No reason for me to delay your visit, see!" He motioned towards a door on the left. "He's in there, yes, just try not to cause a commotion. Don't want the police showing up, heh. The code will be nine-oh-nine-oh." The host put on a fake smile and eyed us in fear, hoping we'd quickly leave him alone.

Villin turned slightly and glanced at me. I interpreted it as 'follow me, time to investigate', or something to that extent. We walked a short distance to the destination; when we arrived at the door, I could hear terrible noises coming from within.

I could hear a woman crying—no, not just crying, she was sobbing. Jester was having sex with her, and it didn't seem like she liked it. This place wasn't just a regular brothel; now I understood what the man meant by 'rent'. You could rent a person here to do whatever you so please. My anxiety started to wash over me again—but it was crushed under a much stronger feeling. It was unexpected; I felt *anger*. We had to stop Jester, and quick. The women were being sold off as property. They once walked free, were normal citizens of Trojan; but now, they were simply objects, enslaved by this criminal gang.

Villin was staring at me with an eyebrow raised. She said, "You kinda froze there for a second. I guess I'd be uncomfortable seeing naked people too, for the first time. Well, we're going to enter now."

I mentally shook my head, trying to clear my mind of thoughts. I had to think quickly depending on the situation that was in that room. Was Jester armed? How dangerous was he? Did he have bodyguards nearby?

Villin inputted the code into the door's lock and then pushed it open. Inside the small, hazy, circular room was Jester, who was on top of a young woman. The girl was crying softly, but not making too much noise by now. Jester was going in hard; I don't think he had noticed that we'd come in.

Villin ran over and kicked him off the poor

girl. She went into her combat stance, whole body lowered, her right hand on her nodachi, ready to strike.

"Jester the Maniac, you're under arrest. Give up and leave here alive, or resist and leave here without your head."

Villin spoke very matter-of-factly—without any hesitation whatsoever. *Something I couldn't do,* I thought.

Jester scrambled back on all fours, naked and all, then stood up, his private parts clearly visible.

"What the HELL is this? Can't you at least wait until I'm done?" he growled, clearly angry. "Well? At least wait 'til a man is done, will you?" Jester's scowl slowly turned into concern, as he realized that Villin had one hand on her sheath and the other on the hilt. The young woman on the floor whimpered and curled up into a ball, glad that the ordeal had temporarily stopped.

"Ten seconds. Make up your mind," spoke Villin, still at the ready. Jester slowly edged towards his belongings. Perhaps getting dressed and willing to give himself up—after all, he had no choice right now.

"Fine, fine. I need to dress though, so could you two leave for a moment? I'm asking nicely," said Jester, suddenly in a pleading voice. He didn't seem genuine, I thought. Nonetheless, Villin appeared to concede, giving way.

"Alright. One minute to dress, no more," stated Villin. She relaxed and stood up straight, then turned around. She glanced at me and said, "When he's done changing, we take him in. Kaz, let's go."

However, I was reluctant to go. A man with that large of a bounty wouldn't just give himself up that quickly, would he? As unsure as I was, I followed Villin out of the room. The main thing I was worried about was the young woman on the floor. I shouldn't worry about her right now, though, because she was safe... at the moment. With Jester changing and then leaving, she should be okay; at least temporarily.

We waited for around ten seconds before I heard the door begin to open. Well, I thought, this wasn't too bad. There was no fight, I didn't have to see any gore. That was until the door opened. Jester had only his pants on, but in his hands was a large pistol. He had it pointed right at Villin.

She noticed it right away and dodged in time. The bullet streaked over her head, slamming into the wall far behind her. Villin quickly swung out her nodachi with a diagonal cut upwards, causing the supersonic whip to vibrate the lobby. Jester didn't have time to shoot again; his body slumped to the floor, spilling out blood. His head was separated from his body, rolling around on the floor. I could only look at it for a moment—it was too disgusting to look at, and I couldn't stomach the scene.

Villin took out her phone from her pocket,

then started to scan Jester's now deceased body. When she was satisfied, she put the phone back in her pocket. She turned to me and said, "We're done here. Let's go."

I turned my head back to the room, eyes skipping over the bloody scene as fast as possible. The young woman was still there, whimpering. As Villin started to leave, I grabbed her arm.

"Villin, what about the human? The girl." I said, unsure of what to do. Villin turned back and looked at her. She shrugged.

"Up to you, Kaz."

Villin didn't seem to care about humans at all. I, on the other hand, didn't know why... but I did.

I walked over to the girl; but each step was harder than the last, as this person was a stranger— and you know how that's going to work out. I just couldn't talk to her. I wanted to help this human, but my social ineptitude was hampering me every step of the way. Villin, seeing this pitiful sight, sighed, then walked over to me, gently nudging me aside. She then kneeled down next to the girl.

"We're here to help. What's your name?"

–

The young woman's name was Rudy, and she had been captured a few days ago by some gang members. She didn't know who they were, as they all had masks on, covering their identity. As I also wore a mask, she was deathly afraid of me. It took Villin a while to calm her down, but when she did, she told us more. She came from the city of Nordt, on Ranktel of the Mscrhmer system (a new system I'd have to look up). She was walking in the dark during the night when the thugs had captured her. They transported her all the way here and got paid a handsome fee. In this place, the 'Bar of Kings' as it was known, she learned that she would be prostituted until someone bought her outright. That could happen the first time, the second time, or... it might never happen. The choices she had, in any case, were all bad. She had been working for a few days already, and Jester was her fifth patron. The other girls outside, she explained, were in her situation as well.

Villin turned to me. She said, "We can save her, Kaz. But what about the others? Will you save them?"

I stepped back outside the room and looked around. There were three other girls visible, standing in front of their doors. The host was pacing around nervously, staring at the blood pooling around Jester's body, or perhaps his head, which had stopped rolling a few seconds into its untimely separation. I went back into the room to speak with Villin, my stomach racing. I said, "We have to."

But deep in my mind, I still wasn't sure if I could help them.

CHAPTER 6 — SPLITTING PATHS

———

After the Eviel incident, Arcus had flown away in his spaceship, scared for his life. With his Technique completely depleted, Villin would easily defeat him. He had to go somewhere far away to rest and recuperate. Mikalev was relatively unharmed from the incident, but was also scared of Villin, especially if she and Hardt were to team up. They plotted a course for the farthest star system— the TCP system.

TCP is a three star system. It is made up of the stars Tor, Cor and Pyro. Pyro is by far the largest, being larger than the other two dwarf stars combined. It is reddish-orange colour, while the others are red-brown in colour. The inhabited planet is named Argona. It is a brown-yellow planet, mostly filled with desert and dirt. Far from the general location of the rest of civilization, the TCP system would be a good fit for Arcus. The chances of Villin or Hardt finding them would be very difficult, especially in such a remote region of the galaxy.

–

They landed in the middle of seemingly nowhere. There were sand dunes and naught else all around them. For as far as the eye could see, there was no sign of human activity. Arcus came out of his ship, laying out on the desert floor; the three stars shone on him, dazzling in his reflective armour, warming his body. Mikalev stood on top of the ship, looking around. He could see nothing but sand for as far as the planet's curvature would allow.

"Ain't nobody here, Arc. We'll be fine, I s'-pose," mentioned Mikalev, still scanning the horizon. Arcus shifted slightly in his position, moving around a few grains of the hot sand. The feeling of warmth from the ground was pleasant, and he wanted to get the maximum amount of heat onto his body.

"Er, Arc-sir? What does take'n over the universe mean, anyway?" Mikalev pondered. He jumped down from the roof and onto the sandy ground, hoping that by going closer to Arcus he could wring an answer out of him. Arcus, his eyes still closed, explained what he meant.

"You see, Mikalev, it could mean anything. Do what you wish, what makes you want to continue. For me, I'll avenge our kind... I'll be unstoppable. I'll make them fear my name. Now, what about you, Mik? What do you want to do?" said Arcus. Mikalev did not immediately answer—for he did not know the answer to that question. He scrambled his mind, trying to figure out what he really wanted to do.

"I dunno... I mean, killing fleshies sounds

fun and all, but I'm not sure that would be some'n I could do every day, ya know?" said Mikalev, still trying to find an answer. Killing wasn't exactly fun for him. The events at Eviel had more than fulfilled the desires he had.

—

"Oh, that's nice—nice and meaty," Arcus said. He circled a family, the members huddled together in terror. Mikalev sat nearby, watching. Every time Arcus killed more people, he felt more sick. Mikalev didn't really enjoy it. It wasn't that he felt sad that Arcus killed them, he just didn't exactly find it entertaining. Arcus then sliced up the family in a flash, reducing them to red piles of meat that spurted out blood. He hung his greatsword over their dead bodies, coating it with more blood. When he was satisfied with the amount of blood that covered his blade, he raised his weapon above his head, then drank the red liquid that dripped into his mouth.

"Eh, Arc… I just ain't happy. I need something to do that I like, ya know?" said Mikalev, watching Arcus' cleaning ritual. Arcus lowered his greatsword and looked at Mikalev.

"Then leave, Mik. No one is forcing you to stay with me. If you can't enjoy the simple pleasures of avenging our kind, then... well, are you really worthy of being a machine?" Arcus retrained his eyes on his greatsword and continued to lick his blade clean.

Mikalev had to make a decision. Would he stay by Arcus' side and kill humans in degrading ways, or would he leave and find his own happiness?

Mikalev stood up and then cleared his throat. His decision was made. He said, "Arc... I'm gonna leave and find som'n else to do. Don't call me a coward, now..."

He hesitated. His whole life, Arcus had led the way. He didn't know what he was going to do. But maybe this was a good thing; a good change. He would take control of his life and perhaps find what he was looking for. Arcus, now finished cleaning his greatsword, sheathed it, then looked towards Mikalev. These would be the last words Mikalev would hear from him in a long, long time.

"Follow your own path, Mik. You will hear of me again, when I become a legend."

CHAPTER 7 — FRIENDSHIP

———

We were travelling back to Earth to turn in the bounty. Even as I sat and watched the universe go by, I still felt ashamed. In the end, it was Villin who talked to them. I couldn't do much but stand by, too scared to say a word. She managed to get them on the ship and we returned them to their homes promptly. It was a long few days, but well worth it to see their families' reaction. Of course, it was all them hugging Villin and thanking her. I just stood somewhere in the back—lucky for me, I guess, for I didn't have to communicate with anyone.

–

I found myself in the empty room once again, trying

to use Technique. Swing as hard as I might, nothing would happen. The terrible thought came back to mind. What if I couldn't use Technique? What if... *the defect*—I shook my head and went back to swinging. I wouldn't give up, not with so much power on the line. I wanted to be powerful. I wanted to be able to protect the person closest to me—

Villin strutted into the room and stared at me. I stopped swinging and stared back. I couldn't tell what was on her mind. Here I was, swinging my greatsword wildly in an empty room. Did she think I was crazy?

"Trying to use your Technique, Kaz? Not so easy, is it?" said Villin. As always, she somehow knew what I was thinking. She walked over and grabbed my arm.

"Close your eyes," she said. I did as she instructed, hoping that she could somehow magically force me to obtain my Technique.

"Now, think of your purpose. What you've

been put in this universe to do. Concentrate on it," she said. Furrowing my brows, I thought for but a moment. I didn't expect it to come to me so quickly, but my mind figured it out in an instant.

"You've made up your mind, Kaz. Now open your eyes, wield your Technique," said Villin. She let go of my arm and took a few steps back. Her uncanny ability to read my thoughts was making me feel uneasy. If she could really read my mind, then she would know that... no, that wasn't possible. She simply has extremely powerful compute abilities, such that she could predict the most probable thing on my mind.

Villin spoke, interrupting my thoughts. "Kaz, I cannot read minds. Now use your Technique."

I was startled once again, but composed myself quickly. Now was time to see if I could harness the power of my Technique.

I lifted my greatsword and looked at it. No

glow in sight. *But perhaps...* I swung the blade horizontally in a fast motion. A faint trail of grey light appeared after the blade, then disappeared quickly. I couldn't believe it—I had control of the higher dimension!

—

I didn't know much about it, the higher dimension. But Villin gave me a lengthy rundown. The most basic usage of Technique is considered as 'passive'. It's always there, in other words. For example, when I sheath my greatsword, the blade disappears in my pocket. I didn't have to do anything—the higher dimension was already at work. Another passive is my armour. Surrounding my entire body is a 'layer' of Technique. I'm not sure how to describe it, but it walls off my body when my armour detects damage, protecting me from harm. That means the only thing that can damage technique machines are other technique machines; like Arcus, Hardt, or Mikalev.

Now for the hard part—'active' Technique.

These aren't simply automatic, you have to control them manually. For example, you can either leave your weapon in the third dimension, or imbue it with Technique and increase its strength infinitely. Nothing in the third dimension can affect objects in the higher dimension normally, so 'coating' weapons with Technique will make them indestructible. The most advanced part of active Techniques, however, is entering the higher dimension itself. By doing so, one can seemingly teleport around at incredible speeds. Villin said it's like taking a shortcut; the higher dimension has another axis to it, allowing us to cross the third dimension quickly. This would take more training to master, as I couldn't get it down correctly on the first day.

The trickiest part is that no one can see the higher dimension. As we're normally three-dimensional beings, it's not possible. Yet five of us can control it; the power we wielded was immense. For me, I wasn't sure what I would do once I had fully mastered my abilities. I am physically strong, sure, but the unusual defect I had was crippling. What would I do if I didn't have Villin to guide me? Thinking about it, I would probably be on a dwarf planet, in the middle of nowhere, doing nothing— except hiding from civilization.

—

As we played a nonillion Elo chess game in the game room, I thought back to the start. Compared to then, I wasn't too nervous around her anymore. With time, I might stop being nervous altogether. But I couldn't imagine that at all; it was too foreign. It was something I didn't have any memory of. All I had known was being nervous all the time.

I did sleep in a bed now, not the cot in the storage room. It was in a room beside Villin's. It had no furnishings; it was just plain and grey. It wasn't bad, it just felt empty. It soon became 'night'. As I lay in my bed, something particular came to mind.

Villin's left arm. It's made of chromiq-carbon. Yes, we are machines—I know that inside, I'm probably some weird mesh of chromiq-carbon and other composites. But her arm didn't look like it was part of her originally. Thinking about it, the only thing that could damage us was Technique. So, it was probably Arcus who did it... if so, she hadn't told me about another fight with Arcus. Or maybe it was during the Eviel incident? But that couldn't be, because I had shielded her and Hardt... unless somehow I didn't shield her enough, and her arm was destroyed. *I should ask her about it later,* I thought. *Right now, I feel tired.*

—

The next day, we arrived back at Bastea, on Earth. I followed Villin as she walked towards the bounty office. I kept my head down, as usual, careful not to look at anyone. '*If I can't see them, they can't see me,*' or something like that. I know that it wasn't true, but it sure seemed to trick my mind into believing it.

At the bounty office was the man at the counter who wore the cowboy hat. He was the same person we'd got the bounty from. Seeing us, he looked up.

"Well, well, well, look what we have here!" said the man. Villin did something on her phone to process the bounty. The man typed something into his computer, before talking to Villin again. He asked, "So, ya want it physical or digital?"

Villin motioned with her hand, still holding her phone. He caught on.

"Ah, digital. The correct way."

He went back to his computer and typed away some more. It wasn't long until Villin glanced at me, signalling that we were done here. I followed her out the door, and back into the bustling city of Bastea.

—

I dreaded these shopping excursions, but I had no

choice. I dutifully followed her to every shop, until we reached the lady's area. I had now become stricken with fear; I couldn't enter with her, but I also couldn't just stay out here, all alone.

"Kaz, stay here. I'll be back soon," Villin said, walking towards a shop. Well, the decision was made, and now I had to stand around doing nothing. Seconds went by, but it already felt like minutes. I felt the wind breeze by, blowing cool air throughout the city, carrying the sounds of nearby shoppers. People walked past me, talking about their everyday excursions. I kept my head down, hoping no one would pay attention to me. *Just walk by, ignore me,* I thought. *Villin, hurry up. I can't stand this much longer.* Yet it had only been a minute when my worst fear would shatter my momentary comfort.

"Hello? Excuse me?" asked a young man. He was in front of me; clearly, he was talking to me. I slowly lifted my head. I was right—he was staring at me.

"Um, can you help me?" he asked, again. He seemed anxious, fidgety. I had to make a decision now. Should I help him, and get this over with as fast as possible? Should I do nothing, and look incredibly awkward? Or should I run away from him, avoiding the problem, but also looking more awkward? The answer was clear.

"What do you need help with?" I mumbled. *I sound nervous, as usual. I can't ever get that thought out of my mind.*

"Oh, my neighbour has been bothering me lately. I'd like him removed, if you know what I mean. I'll pay handsomely."

I stared at him blankly. He wanted me to... kill someone? I stammered out a response. "You want me to kill your neighbour?" I asked, confused. I was looking at his face, trying to figure out what he was thinking.

"Yea, it should be easy. He's pretty old, so

he won't put up a fight, eh? Haha... ha," remarked the young man, an awkward grin appearing on his face. I looked around. Was no one else hearing this? Apparently not. Everyone else was focused on their everyday activities and couldn't pay mind to a random conversation by a clothing store.

I turned my head back to the man, who was still fidgeting. "No, I won't kill him, not even for money," I stated. I hoped he would leave me alone. My anxiety was through the roof, but other emotions were welling up inside me as well. Like sadness that this person would want his neighbour dead, and anger that he would come to me, talk to me, and make my anxiety skyrocket.

"What's the deal? Ain't you one of them assassins?" he said, confused. That's when it hit me— he thought I was an assassin. Was it because of my mask? My armour? Something else? It made me second-guess how I looked. If he thought I was a hitman, could that mean other passersby thought I was one as well? Did they think I was sitting outside the store, waiting for someone to hire me?

"No, I am not an assassin. I am waiting for my… friend to finish shopping."

I had managed to get off a long sentence without stuttering in between words. My voice wasn't shaky, either. My anger gave me confidence, I guess. The man then shrugged, mumbled an apology, then walked away. The ordeal was over; it had only been two minutes, yet it felt like an eternity. As my anger subsided, and the drone of the crowd became louder again, I began feeling more nervous once more. The thoughts that people were staring at me had now increased with the fact that they might think I was something I was not, or doing something I was not doing. I kept my head down and focused on breathing.

Breathe in, breathe out.
Breathe in, breathe out…

It wasn't working; the drone of the crowd

was growing louder, and with it, my fear.

"Kaz? We're going now."

Villin was standing in front of me, unaware of the perilous situation I had just survived. I nodded, not sure if I should speak of what happened. The only thought on my mind was returning to the safety of the ship; far removed from the city.

–

We were now headed to the city of Eve, on planet Volke. Their star system, Tau system, was the closest system to the center of the galaxy. As such, it was the place most likely to have all the dangerous bounties available—and therefore where all the top bounty hunters hung out. As we slowly crept our way there, I felt dread come back once again. *More bounties means leaving the ship again, which means going out into the city...* I shuddered at the thought. The events of earlier today still traumatized me, and I didn't want to be in such a situation ever again.

CHAPTER 8 – A DEADLY PLAN

———

Arcus had already assassinated five bounty hunters that were bound for Van Hire. He was waiting for more when he got the news. It was from Van Hire; the bounty was recalled. Arcus was both pleased and displeased at the news. It meant he was successful; his mission was complete. It also meant that his steady stream of feisty prey would cease. Sure, he could kill civilians. But what fun was there in that? They would scream, cry, then die, all too quickly. They couldn't put up a fight. Maybe the planetary police or army would come, but they were weak as well. A hundred of them might as well be one. It only took one blade swing and they'd all fall, anyway.

But the top-ranked bounty hunters—especially those after a high-priced bounty. They could actually dodge a few blows. They could put up a fight. Now, they couldn't touch Arcus, but it was fun to toy with them and watch them struggle to survive. They always started off cocky, thinking they were the best. After all, they were the hotshots in their own right, usually ranked in the top one hundred. But it wouldn't be long before Arcus whittled them down to nothing. They'd always beg for their lives. They'd plead and plead. At a certain point, it was no longer fun. At that point, Arcus would kill them.

Arcus had lost count of how many people he'd killed a long time ago (*author's note: at this moment, more than a dozen billion*). Killing wasn't giving him the satisfaction he had one obtained from it. He wanted something more. A grander plan had started to form in his mind; his original ideas of complete human eradication started to take hold once more. Arcus had the power and the drive; the only thing that had stopped him before was that he knew that somewhere out there, somewhere in the cosmos, were Villin and Kazjivo. They'd surely come to stop him if he proceeded with galactic domination. But then again, he hadn't heard from or seen them for a long time. Perhaps Kazjivo had never woken up. Or maybe Kazjivo woke up and killed Villin? Either way, it was time for Arcus to act. He was stronger than ever now and thirsty for more.

Arcus looked in the mirror. He still looked the same as all those years ago; a charming man with a wicked smile. *It's all mine—and no one can stop me!*

—

The Volkean officer rushed into the room, out of breath. In the large room sat a large table with a dozen elders sitting around it. They curiously turned towards the newcomer, some glaring, others with a look of concern on their faces.

"Speak up, officer," stated one of the dozen. He was old, wore glasses, and dressed in smart attire. He was the leader of Volke: Sir Ramus. Sat around him, leaders of other planets. This was no ordinary meeting.

"A ton of famous and top-ranked bounty hunters have fallen trying to chase Van Hire, my liege. A spy we sent following the latest one figured out why..." The officer paused for a moment, catching his breath. Once he gathered himself, he proceeded.

"The person killing them all is Arcus Aytfri."

Gasps and murmurs followed the announcement. The leaders of the round table looked at each other, uncertain of what to do. Sir Ramus raised his hand, commanding silence. As the sounds of whispers died away, he spoke.

"Alright, alright, calm down everyone. While this news is certainly most distressing, it does also mean he's contained in Dos, for now. Officer, you may take your leave."

The Volkean officer bowed and then left, leaving the table silent. Then, the leader of Dos, a Lady Angin, spoke up angrily.

"Contained? What do you mean? He must be contained somewhere else. Trojan is already corrupted by Van Hire and his crew. We can't have that devil in here as well!"

"As long as he remains in Dos, the rest of us will be fine. We shall send more troops to handle the situation of Van Hire in the meantime," said Sir Ramus, softly.

"Oh, so we are sacrifices now? I demand you at least put the bounty back up for Van Hire—" sputtered Lady Angin. She was quickly interrupted by Sir Ramus.

"And what? Send more to their deaths? The

top ranks of bounty hunters have been depleted. If we lose more, the rest of the galaxy will suffer. No, we must take a different course of action. We'll send troops, like I said. It WILL be contained. If you want to set up your own bounty, go for it. But there will be no more talks on such matters for now."

"Hmph... if you'd like to pitch in, I'd like to hear voices, now," thundered Lady Angin. She stood up, waiting for her peers to join in. The other members sat quietly, looking at one another, but no one made a motion. Lady Angin scowled at them.

"You cowards! You'd let another planet suffer to keep your own safe. I pray you never ask Trojans for help when the time comes." She stormed out of the meeting room, her peers still silent.

"I... I will help with another bounty, per-haps..." stammered out Sir York, the leader of Earth. He stood up, bowed, then followed the path of Lady Angin. The rest of the leaders looked at each other, seeing who else would follow. When moments passed, and no one did, Sir Ramus spoke up.

"Now… we must speak of Mr. Aytfri. The one who destroyed Eviel has returned. It will not be long until he bares his face again…"

—

"Cheers! Cheers!" The bar was full of laughter and joyous cries. Van Hire's billion-dollar bounty had been removed, and he and his crew were celebrating it. Hiring Arcus was incredibly successful, if very expensive. Money wouldn't matter if you were dead, however, so it was money well spent.

"One swig fer Sir Arcus, one swig fer Van Hire!" shouted out a pirate. Others raised their mugs and then they started to chug down their alcohol. It was a turn of events from only a short while ago in this bar.

The Bar of Kings was raided a few days ago, and the owner, Jester the Maniac, was brutally

beheaded. All the immediate product was also removed. It wasn't a normal raid either. It didn't
involve the police of Dlli, or the government of Trojan. It was just two bounty hunters. The witnesses to
the raid were sure the hunters looked similar to Arcus. Van Hire didn't really know what to think of it,
but whatever the reason, the bar and trafficking operations were now his. With no leader, Jester's gang
was lost and was eager to join Van Hire's powerful
crew.

Van Hire had asked Arcus to join in the celebration, but Arcus refused, and disappeared soon
after. He was a mysterious man with mysterious
motives. But, as long as you had him in his good
graces, you were safe.

Van Hire, deep in thought, was interrupted
by a pirate.

"Boss, hey boss, want 'nother bottle?"

The pirate stumbled around, very drunk. In
his hand was a bottle of Trojan vodka, the strongest

kind in the galaxy. Van Hire gladly took it and started to chug. The crew started to chant upon seeing their boss join in the merriment.

"Chug! Chug! Chug! Chug! Wooo!"

Van Hire wiped his bearded mouth with his right arm's sleeve. Globs of spittle mixed with vodka flew off and infected the floor. He wore a giant grin on his face and signalled for another bottle. His power was growing, and as long as Arcus was on his side, nothing could stop him.

—

It was night at the Bar of Kings. A huge party had concluded, and the staff was cleaning up. They would have to prematurely close this day.

Swish, swish, swish.

The bartender was wiping down the table Van Hire had sat by. It was heavily stained with all kinds of fluids.

Swish, swish, swish.
Knock, Knock, Knock.

The bartender looked up. There was a patron at the door, knocking. The bartender frowned. He was sure he put up the 'closed' sign. He squinted his eyes to make sure—yep, the sign was there all right. He sighed, stood up, then walked towards the entrance.

"Hey, can ya read? It says close—" the bartender stopped mid-sentence, recognizing the figure outside. "My mistake, Sir Schren! My apologies, you can come in, of course."

As the door opened, the green-clad figure walked in, then motioned for a bottle. The bartender scurried along quickly and retrieved a bottle for him. The figure popped open the bottle and drank slowly before speaking.

"I ain't been in 'ere foreva. Why's it closed this time? And ya seen Arcus recently?"

The bartender shook his head, then said, "It's a really long story, ya sure ya wanna hear it all?"

The figure momentarily stopped drinking to nod his head.

The bartender sighed before beginning.

"Well you see, a week ago, two bounty hunters walked into a bar…"

CHAPTER 9 – MY TERRIBLE DEFECT

⸺

We landed on Eve during the earlier hours of the capital's day cycle. I felt a bit tired, for if I stayed on one planet, it would be evening by now. Villin checked the ship control panels one last time, making sure everything was in order, then activated the deck ramp. As the deck lowered, my anxiety skyrocketed once again.

As usual, I dutifully followed Villin. I knew we were going to the bounty office, but I didn't know where it was. The humans on each planet looked relatively the same. Their attire, however, was always different and varied. The people here seemed quite advanced and wore more modern, simple-looking clothes. *I suppose if your system is near the middle of the galaxy, you'd get lots of trade, and therefore a good economy.* As we neared the bounty office, my fears rose. There was a line leading into the office. Inside, it was crammed with bounty hunters. I didn't know how long it would take to get an order—not to mention the building's inside, which would be packed full of people when the line diminished and we eventually got through.

But my body was becoming numb. My mind, dizzy. There were too many people around me. I had to make my decision now. Would I wait in this line and subject myself to torture? Or would I act now, going against my mind to do nothing? The decision didn't come to me immediately.

My mind struggled to choose one, with each moment passed seeming to slow down time as we walked closer and closer to the office. Either I make my choice now, or be stuck with a terrible option. I grabbed Villin's shoulder, stopping us both.

"Kaz?" she said. She turned to look at me, unsure why I stopped.

"I can't… I won't go," I said. My decision was made; I decided that I had to leave. My numb and barely controllable body, however, wanted to keep the status quo.

I felt something else welt up inside me. *Anger*.

Anger was coursing through me. Villin knew me enough by now. She's smart, too. She clearly knows my struggle, yet she always has me in tow. To the office. To the shops. To me waiting outside the shop.

More so, why would she pull a confused look right now? She was feigning confusion; she was smarter than that, knew better. She had to be toying with me, watching my anguish. In my anger, I felt my anxiety go away, if only ever so slightly. But even so, it gave me courage. It was the surge of confidence I needed to force my legs into action.

I turned around and ran. I ran towards Argua, the only place I knew was safe. People stared at me as I ran, but I didn't care. All I could think of was going home. I didn't look back. It didn't matter, anyway. People might think I'm weird, but they'd forget about it soon anyway. A lot of people run to places for various reasons. Villin, on the other hand, was she mad that I embarrassed her? Would people gossip about why I ran away from her? I didn't know. *I didn't care.*

—

I was out of breath when I reached Argua. It was stationed in a busy port, but I used the higher dimension to travel inside the ship. Inside was quiet and safe. There was no one in here; I could finally relax. *Now, I should prepare for what her excuse is when she comes back...*

"Kazjivo," yelled Villin. She was out of breath—she had followed me. I kept my head down, refusing to look at her. I still felt anger, for some reason.

"Kaz, I'm sorry."

She knelt down to me. Before I could respond, she clutched my head and placed it on her chest. My anger was subsiding, now replaced by embarrassment. *Is she purposely putting me between her...* For now, all I could do was stay in her embrace.

I guess I was childish to think she'd enjoy my suffering. She had helped me through everything so far, letting me learn the world at my own pace; she had always looked after me. I felt foolish to have let my anger get the best of me. I felt bad, but I couldn't express it. I couldn't say anything.

Villin stood up, then held her hand out. I grabbed onto her, and she guided me back to my room. She then went back out, presumably for the bounty—which was today's mission— and waved goodbye. I was left alone for now, thinking about her, and what had transpired.

—

Hours passed by, and I got more and more worried. I had to summon more courage again; I had to go out and find her. *The line couldn't have been that long, could it?* I thought. A little bit of me was relieved I didn't have to stand there, but it was overpowered by the feeling of guilt. The guilt of leaving her alone there. What if something had happened to her? It would've all been my fault. I went through the higher dimension to exit the spaceship.

Outside the ship, I was greeted with darkness. It was nighttime. The streetlights had turned on and a few people were still about, doing whatever they were out to do. I sighed one more time, mustering up courage, then headed for the general direction of the bounty office.

I wandered through the mostly empty streets, following the path I remembered taking earlier with Villin. Once again, there sprung the evil feelings within me. The feeling of anger; of how she was making me do this. Making me walk around cities with her everywhere. I quickly shrugged it off. That was the dark side of me acting up again. I had to ignore the thoughts, otherwise it would consume my mind.

I kept up a brisk pace. Soon, I reached the main shopping district. There, in the center of it all, was the bounty office. It was lit up; still open, I surmised. I walked up to the door and peered through the window. Inside were a few people—but Villin was nowhere in sight. I opened the door and stepped in; as I had thought, Villin was definitely not here. *Where could she be, then?* I started to panic. There was only one person at the counter now, so I went in line. It wasn't long until the person finished up and I could talk to the bounty officer.

"Hello, sir. How may I help you?" said the officer. I blanked out for a second, trying to think of what to say.

"Yes… uh… did you see a lady, uh, named Villin, today?" I asked. I mentally scolded myself for stammering too much.

The officer, not caring about my speaking skills, was quick to respond.

"Why yes! The best bounty hunter in the universe! One can't miss her, I must say. If you're looking for her, she left a few minutes ago, not sure where though," he said.

I muttered out a 'thank you' and then rushed out of the building. Either we passed by each other, or… I didn't know what to think. *Just rush back,* I thought. This time I used my Technique, so I wouldn't waste any time.

—

I used my key to open the ship's deck ramp this time. As it lowered, I heard footsteps rapidly approaching me. As I stepped onto the ramp, I saw Villin standing on the main deck. She rushed down and gave me a soul-crushing hug. I didn't know, but at that moment, she had tears in her eyes.

As I was halfway to the office, Villin had finished getting her bounty. She then used her Technique to rush back to the ship. But when she arrived, I wasn't there. Argua told her that I had gone out, but didn't know where. She then flew up to a vantage point, trying to see where I went. She was afraid that I had run away.

–

I felt like a child. To be fair to me, however, I had only been in existence for over a few months now. Even so... I wanted to be more mature, less dependent on my defective emotions. I had to be.

CHAPTER 10 — A FAMILIAR FACE

I strived to be a stronger person. And so, I would do the dirty work—I would go on a bounty hunt as the lead. Villin was surprised at my suggestion, but she didn't protest. The bounty was $100,000,000, *quite* the large step up from the first bounty. The bounty was for a criminal known as Garvin the Bad. He was wanted for thousands of human trafficking cases and murders across three systems. According to Villin, cameras around the system had not seen him for a few days. That meant we'd have to go on the ground where he was last located, and snoop around.

—

We landed in what Villin said was the most likely place for him to be in. It was in the Kyan Jyan system, on planet KJ4. New planets always awed me, but also gave me the fear of the unknown.

When we landed, Villin unconsciously took the lead and I followed; thankfully, she forgot that I was supposed to lead this mission. She went around asking people if they'd seen Garvin. Many shook their heads, others said nothing, instead just briskly walked away. It was evident that Garvin was around; but because of his apparent presence, no one would say a word.

We soon came upon a bar. Knowing our previous experience at these establishments, she surmised that this one could be one of Garvin's trafficking venues as well. It was well lit and it seemed like many people were in there. Villin motioned me to follow, and we walked in.

The familiar smell of booze hit me as we entered. Another familiar scent pervaded... it was the same smell I had smelt before—a salty smell mixed in with sweat.

There was loud chatter from the bar. People there seemed to be enjoying themselves, indulging in copious amounts of alcohol. As we traversed towards the counter, Villin scanned the entire area, looking for Garvin. I also kept my eyes peeled; then I spotted something that seemed familiar. A man had caught my eye. He was wearing a dark green jacket, the same design that Villin and I had. I couldn't quite remember who that was supposed to be, so I tapped Villin on her shoulder. She turned around, with a questioning look in her eye. I gestured towards the man in green. Villin saw him and froze.

The man wore a dark-green jacket covering heavy armour underneath and had a hood covering his head, with messy hair sticking out. The man was drinking heavily; he hadn't noticed us yet. Villin recognized him, though I couldn't. She pulled me aside, then whispered in my ear.

"That person in the green. He's Mik. Mikalev Schren."

Villin kept her voice low, so the man wouldn't hear her. It made sense now. The man in green was Mikalev; he was one of us. From what I recall, he was the one who helped Arcus.

Mikalev was drinking beer at a table, alone. As he sipped on his bottle, Villin slowly crept towards him. I was obliged to follow. What were we doing next? Villin gave no directions, as she was transfixed on Mikalev. *If he does anything crazy,* I thought, *I'll have to intervene.*

Villin spoke softly. "Mikalev..."

We had reached his table, and we now stood behind him. Mikalev laid down his beer and turned around slowly. His eyes became wide open as he saw Villin. He was surprised.

Mikalev stumbled for words, unsure of the situation he was suddenly thrust into. Finally, something coherent came out of him.

"V-V-Villi?" he said, then continued. "What brings ya 'er? Surely ya can't be fixn' to assassinate me!?"

He seemed drunk, but that couldn't be possible. He wasn't a human, after all. So... he must have been emulating drunkenness. Villin, unfazed by his poor acting, spoke sharply.

"Where's Arcus?" she demanded, glaring at him. Mikalev looked away and muttered something.

"Excuse me?" said Villin. Her tone was getting a bit nasty.

"I haven't seen bossman in a while. If ya ain't 'er ta kill me, then leave my poor soul alone, will ya?" huffed Mikalev. He then lifted his bottle back to his lips and took another long sip.

Villin looked around, then decided to turn her piercing glare back to Mikalev.

"Then what have you been doing, Mik? What about plans of galactic domination?"

Mikalev tried to ignore her, but eventually gave up to her persistent stare.

"Eh… after a while, killing gets quite boring. Ya know, people screaming all the time ain't good for the soul. So I went off and did me own thing." He took a sip of beer, then continued.

"Ya know, random stuff. I tried a job. I tried acting like a human. But it weren't long 'til I found ma calling. It was hanging out in these bars! Wondrous thing, this place is. All the booze you can drink. Any woman you want, you can have—," he suddenly stopped, then looked around. He then looked at Villin. He whispered, "Ya know about the women, right?"

Villin gave a quick nod. He meant the secret back room, where one could pay to spend some time with someone, or pay a large amount to actually buy them. This all related back to Garvin the Bad, our bounty. He was the ringleader of this severe lack of regard for human rights. Very similar to Jester the

Maniac, but I guess Jester was a small fry compared to this guy.

Mikalev rambled on. "Well, that was ma calling! I can have all the women I want, and when I'm done, I drink more booze. This is just the life for me. Forget killing people… I'm fine right 'ere." Mikalev returned back to his beer and took a long gulp, emptying his bottle. He glanced back at us, still standing there. He said, "Well, ya gonna leave a machine alone? My favourite bar got raided a few days ago, and they took the girl I was gonna buy. I ain't in the best mood, right now."

He then froze, as if noticing me for the first time. He tilted his head, looking me up and down, before speaking.

"Kazjivo? Damn, ya woke up finally. Ya remember anything?"

I stood still, unsure whether to speak or not. Taking my silence as an answer, Mikalev continued.

"Well shit, he got brain damage or

somethin'? Damn, well, that'll be disappointin' news for Arc, I guess." Mikalev then turned back to his bottle and continued his drink.

Villin motioned me over, and we walked to a table far away from Mikalev's. She was mulling over what Mikalev had said. After thinking for a while, Villin turned to me and whispered, "Mik might get mad once we bust Garvin. This would be another of his bars temporarily closed; he'll have to find somewhere else. Ah well. We will have to deal with him later. Right now, we need to find Garvin." A waiter came by, but Villin waved him off. She continued. "This is Garvin's main bar. He was last seen entering this building. He also hasn't been seen for the past few days on the cameras that are nearby. You know where I'm going at?"

Villin stared at me. Her violetish-blue eyes pierced into mines... or into my mask, trying to fig-ure out my expression underneath. *I'm probably thinking about that too much again,* I thought. *Mind reading is impossible.* But yes, that would mean chances are he's still in here. Unusual, it would seem... but we had checked all the other places surrounding this area, and had found no sign of him. Maybe he really enjoyed his own services here. He was the boss of the bars, so it wouldn't exactly be outlandish for him to stay overnight... or nights, as it were. Then, Villin stood up, ready to go to the back area; I obliged.

–

We got the code from the bartender, without much hassle, then entered the secret hallway. There were vibrant posters here, unlike Jester's bar's hallway, which was completely plain. The posters were of paintings, but rather than hand-drawn, they seemed to be photos of paintings that were made into posters, which were then hung up here like paintings.

Villin opened the door at the end of the hallway. As expected, we were greeted with a large circular room filled with people. Around the edges of the room were doors, a few decorated with potential *product*. While they tried to not show it, their body language indicated they were under severe duress.

Villin looked around for a special door. One of these rooms should be Garvin's personal room. All the doors looked the same, however. *Probably for security.* After a few moments, Villin frowned. It wasn't going to be easy to find him. She shook her head, then scanned the room in a full 360-degree turn, causing some people in the room to eye her suspiciously.

"Our target—Garvin—is in…"

She turned around once more.

"That room."

She pointed to the door to the immediate right of the hallway door. She said, "An interesting tactic. Instead of in the back, where one would expect it to be, it's right in the front. Let's go, shall we?"

As Villin headed towards the door, I couldn't help but notice the room's host looking at us. He started to walk towards us at a brisk pace, clearly wary of us.

"Oh! Hey, hey folks, you can't enter that room! That one's not available at the moment. No lady is at the door—that means it's in session! Ha ha."

The businessman smiled at us uneasily and made a gesture to another room that was available. He said, "Look at this one, the lady here is still a virgin! I highly recommend it. What say you?"

Villin looked at him, looked at the lady by the door, then back to Garvin's room door. She was making a split-second decision. Whatever she did, I would have to back her up, be it breaking the door or worse.

In one fluid motion, Villin went into her combat pose, hand on nodachi handle, then swung right through Garvin's door. In Garvin's room sat Garvin, drinking beer with a few of his men. He only had a split second to react in surprise before Villin rushed in, releasing a wide slash, decapitating all the men at the table.

The host's mouth went wide open and he stumbled backwards. It looked like he was ready to run. I had to act now—should I kill him, and stop him from yelling? Or should I let him go, let him yell, and perhaps be forced to kill more people? It didn't matter—before I could act, Villin teleported behind him and cut the host in half.

The sound of the door collapsing was quite loud. Definitely loud enough for everyone in the main room to hear. And hear they did. The patrons ran for cover, screaming at the horrific sight, and Garvin's crew stood still in disbelief. Villin saw their mouths gaping and wasted no time, killing them as well. In a moment, Garvin and all his men had fallen. Our bounty was already complete.

"I assume you want to rescue the humans—am I wrong, Kaz?" questioned Villin, while flicking blood off her blade.

"You aren't wrong. Let's help them."

Patrons started to flee the scene, running out the hallway. Villin went to the nearest girl and started to speak with her. Once again, I wanted to help. But I felt paralyzed with fear. I couldn't talk to strangers... even ones that needed my help. I wasn't a leader, I didn't know what to do, what to say.

But I couldn't be weak.

These people needed help right now; more so than my anxiety needed to be calmed down. I am supposed to be strong.

I must be strong.

—

I had only helped one person when Villin had gathered the rest of them. The food supplies and clothes in our ship came in handy, as the trafficked humans had a great appetite and no real clothing of their own. While they were on board, my anxiety stayed at a constant state of 'terrified'. They were grateful for us, and they kept thanking us profusely. I guess it made sense, but I couldn't handle it. I stayed by Argua the whole time, talking to the yellow glob as an excuse to stay away from everyone.

To make more room for them, Villin let a few into my room. This meant I would be sleeping in Villin's room with her. That made me uneasy and embarrassed at the same time; I didn't know how I would do it. She insisted I get the bed and she could sleep on the floor, but I refused. I brought over the old cot from the storage room, explaining to her that I had spent years sleeping on it, and a few days wouldn't hurt.

Regarding my room, I didn't know how I could sleep on my bed again, now that it had been covered with human bacteria. I shivered at the thought; I was very germaphobic, and everything had to be clean. *Probably another part of my defect.*

I guess the old cot I woke up from would have to do from now on until I could get a new bed. The only person I had ever come in direct contact with was Villin, but she felt... normal. I didn't feel dirty when she touched me. If anything, she always felt cleaner than me, for some reason.

We travelled through the night, visiting various cities to get all the victims back to their homes. Once again, I stayed in the back, just watching from a distance. I watched as Villin talked to their families, and they shook her hand profusely. It warmed my heart to see them go back to their loved ones, their family, their friends. After we finished up, an unusual thought crossed my mind.

Who is Villin, to me?

CHAPTER 11 – CONFIDENCE

———

After that adventure, Villin set her eyes back on Tau system. In there was another planet that she liked visiting, for its high-end shopping district: Ceti, the sister planet to Volke. Like Volke, Ceti rotated around the same star. It was the same shape and size. Unlike Volke, however, Ceti had a gigantic ring going across the planet diagonally. The most startling thing about Ceti was that it was on Volke's same path around the star—except that it was on the other side. They could never collide, however, as Volke was further ahead and therefore always 'on top' or 'ahead' of Ceti in space, due to the rotation of Tau around Sagittarius A.

The previous bounty (worth 100 million, re-member?) gave a large enough chuck of money that Villin decided it was time to relax. A large amount would be an understatement, though. The amount we had earned during the week was enough to last more than any human's lifetime. It was far more than we could ever need, and I hadn't even seen Vil-lin's bank account yet, so who knows how much more she keeps in there.

We headed towards the capital city of Ceti: Taurus. Skyscrapers dominated the skyline. Air and ground vehicles of all kinds zipped around the city, making it a dazzling sight. Ceti was as advanced as Volke, the most advanced civilization. Whereas Volke's capital Eve was full of vibrant colour and modernistic curves, Taurus' buildings were very in-dustrial in design. They were mostly grey in shade and blocky in shape.

"No parking, no parking! Help!" said Argua. The yellow glob was spinning around rapidly in panic.

The port we were entering seemed completely full; I did a quick scan but couldn't find any parking spots. I looked at Villin, and her face was concentrated as she looked for parking.

Her eyes were scanning intensely, focused towards a corner of the port. In only a moment, she found a suitable empty spot.

The scale of the port was enormous. As far as I could see, from one corner to the next, there were rows upon rows of spacecraft. Thousands of people were bustling around, and multiple spaceships were leaving and entering the busy port.

We were headed to a tall building where Villin owned a condo. Even from a distance, I could see that the building was the tallest around. It soared above all the other skyscrapers, dominating the skyline.

To get there, we walked through the lower

section of the city. It was dark, as sunlight was blocked by overhead bridges and roads. Looking around, it became clear that this area wasn't as wealthy as the upper levels. People weren't dressed fashionably, and the few vehicles that did pass by looked like relics of the past.

There were fewer people here, though, so that was why we chose this route. I kept my face facing forward, pretending to be confident. Walking through unknown streets in an unknown world, I felt nervous; but I would overcome it. Hopefully.

—

A man wearing a torn white shirt abruptly bumped into Villin, then waved an apology.

"M'bad," he muttered. Then, in one swift, rehearsed action, his left hand brushed onto Villin's breast and squeezed.   Unfortunately for him, her chest armour completely blocked the attempt, so his hands only touched metal.

I reacted.

I stepped forward, drew my fist back, then punched him square in his face. He flew back a few meters before slamming into the ground and rolling with audible thumps. Nearby citizens stopped what they were doing, and stared at the commotion.

I ran over to the man, who was loudly grunting in pain. I lifted him up by his shirt collar and into the air. His face was bloody, his nose now nonexistent. His eyes were swollen and purple; one was completely shut and the other opened slightly as I lifted him up.

"P-please sir, I meant no harm! 'Twas an honest mistake, I promise!" he shouted. His voice was shaky. He was terrified. But what did he expect would happen? Did he think he could do that and get away?

I let go of his collar, dropping him down, then kicked his crotch for good measure. He screamed in pain and buckled to his knees.

"Ugh… have mercy! I beg you," whimpered

the man. He was on the ground, making weird noises. "Me balls… they're gone... they're gone!" he cried out, clutching his crotch area.

Then, I felt a hand on my shoulder. It was Villin.

"Let's go. He's learned his lesson," she said. I nodded, and we went back on our journey to the condo. As I glanced back, everyone in the area was frozen, still staring at me.

—

To get to our building, we had to go up quite a few steps from the lower level to ground level. More people and vehicles seemed to appear exponentially the higher we progressed.

When we reached the top layer, the sun shone brightly down at us, and off of the reflective surfaces of the surrounding skyscrapers. It was almost blinding at times. The top layer was three layers higher than the ground region; if you fell down, it would be a nasty fall. It was a very noisy and busy place. The building Villin's condo was located in was now very visible; a giant tower amongst many giant towers. We had crossed busy crosswalks and gone through various shortcuts before we finally arrived at the base of the building.

There were tons of people moving in and out the building, like a swarm of ants going to and fro a fallen apple. Many vehicles, land and air, were parked in the large parking lot that preceded the entrance. Villin glanced back at me, not sure if I could handle it.

"Let's go," I said, reassuring her. I knew that going in there was going to be difficult, but I as long as I had Villin with me, I could do it. I could feel myself changing with each passing moment. It wasn't much, but as time progressed, I began to feel slightly more confident.

–

Villin led us to the main lobby area. The people inside were dressed professionally, most presenting fancy suits and ties. We directed ourselves toward the elevators. Luckily for us, one was already on the ground floor, with no one inside.

"Let's see… over here," mumbled Villin. She pressed the buttons labelled nine then two. Her condo was on the ninety-second floor; we were going to go up very high.

As the floors whizzed by, I started to think about heights. Was I scared of them? I wasn't too sure. I never really looked out the window of the ship when we lifted off, and I didn't pay much attention to the planet surface once we were landing. It always seemed like the ship was a stable and secure place. Sunlight, which was coming out through the windows of the main lobby (which stretched to the roof) and into the elevator window, brought me back to reality. We were now very high up, and moving very fast. I tried not to look down, but curiosity got the best of me. I looked down and felt dizzy. My sense of balance seemed to disappear, and it felt as if my lungs rose to my throat.

Villin put her hand on my shoulder, comforting me. "Scared of heights? Just look forward, not down," she said, nonchalantly. It wasn't the words that calmed me down. Moreso the fact that she was basically holding me steady with one arm.

—

The rest of the journey in the elevator was a blur. Sometimes I think too much, and in the process, forget what I was thinking about.

When the elevator door opened, we were greeted by a clean hallway that smelled like roses, either recently cleaned or sprayed with tons of air freshener. Villin walked past a few nondescript doors until she reached one with a small 'five' labelled on it. She then unlocked the door—this was her condo. The room was large but plain. The interior was cascaded in sunlight, as it was still noon, diffusing the soothing amber light inside. There was a large couch in the middle, with a small television set adjacent to it. To the right was a kitchen with a rectangular center table; it was quite dusty and didn't seem to have been used in forever. To the left of the room were some doors; what I presumed were bedrooms and everything else.

I took off my metal boots and stood awkwardly by the doorway. I didn't know what to do, and Villin took notice.

"You can sit down on the couch. There's an ancient TV there if you want to watch anything," she said. I walked over and sat on the couch, sinking deep into its plush cushions. There was a dusty remote on the table in front of the couch; I wasn't very tempted to watch anything, but maybe I'd look at the news later. I glanced out the large windows to my left, gazing at the neighbouring sky rises; the sunlight streaming into the room made window dust visible, catching my attention. The particles floated down, ever so slowly, towards the floor.

—

A day had passed since we arrived at Villin's condo in Taurus. I had naught much to do, so I took up an old notepad Villin had laying around and started to write. I was writing about my journey from when I woke up, to whenever the notepad would run out of space.

It wasn't long until I remembered I had to buy a new bed. Villin had already left, gone shopping. I would have to do this alone. With fear taking over my mind, I decided to keep writing in the notepad.

A few hours passed sitting in the condo. After a while, though, I got bored. I then eventually mustered up the courage to buy the bed. I couldn't sleep on that old cot forever.

—

I wasn't prepared for this adventure. I didn't have a phone; I didn't even ask Villin where the stores were. But I had already started, and I wasn't going to give up so easily. So, I wandered through the streets of the upper levels, but after a long time searching, found no furniture stores. Eventually, I found myself in the lower streets of Taurus; the shops here had more everyday stuff—it seemed more promising. Soon, I found myself in the same area Villain and I had originally walked through; the place where I beat up the pervert. It was evening now, and the light was even dimmer than it was before. Red-lit street lamps dotted the street, giving a bit of light for the citizens of this level.

"Sir, wait please!" someone called out.

I turned around, caught off guard. It was an older lady holding a basket of various foods. I wasn't sure what was going to happen. Was she the wife of the guy I punched earlier? Was I going to have to punch *more* humans?

"Please, accept this. I can't thank you enough for teaching that creep Gus a lesson." She held the basket out towards me, inviting me to take it. So 'Gus' must have been the pervert in the white shirt. I guess he was trouble in this community, and I stopped him for good.

The lady ran back to her house, leaving me standing on the street with a basket in my hands. It was a kind gesture, but I didn't need to eat food. I wondered what I would do with the basket; throw it away? No, that would be wasteful. I didn't want to hold onto it, though.

As I continued my journey to find a mattress store, I saw a man dressed in rags, sitting by the side of a store. Approaching him, I could see that he was homeless. I looked at the basket I was given. *This would be much more useful for him than for me,* I thought. Yet, I still sighed; this simple journey already included too much human interaction. I walked up to him, hoping to get over this quickly.

He looked up, hearing my footsteps. I held the basket out for him to take.

"Oh, thank you. I appreciate your kindness,"

he said. I muttered a 'you're welcome' and then continued my journey.

—

In the end, I wasn't able to find the store. But never to worry; Villin, done with her shopping trip, had actually bought a bed and fitted it on the spaceship while I was on my little excursion. Before going to sleep, I was back to scribbling away at the notepad. The pages were filling up fast, though, so I wasn't sure how much more of my story I could write down. *The notebook is almost done. That'll be enough for today.*

CHAPTER 12 – UPRISING

———

Arcus entered the bar and walked up to the counter. The bartender was serving other patrons, but as soon as he saw Arcus, he ignored the patrons, much to their displeasure, and went up to Arcus.

"Er, Arcus... the usual—it's under repair right now. You heard the news, right?" said the bartender, nodding solemnly. Yes, Arcus had heard the news. Garvin and his main posse were killed at this bar by two bounty hunters. The one who killed Garvin was a female that had a metal arm. Arcus had an eerie suspicion about who that one was but didn't know who the other could be.

Arcus furrowed his brow. Even with Garvin

dead, someone else should take control. Business should be up and running. Arcus wanted the usual, and he wanted it now.

"Arcus, it's not ready, really—"

Arcus pushed past the bartender and smashed through the secret door. He walked through the hallway, pissed. Whatever he wanted, he got.

—

Standing in the center of the main room were a group of men arguing with a scruffy-looking man who wore green. *Could it be…? No,* thought Arcus. Mikalev was probably a hermit living alone in a forest on some remote planet. But as he got closer, it became more apparent that this was, in fact, his old right hand Mikalev Schren.

Mikalev was arguing with the new boss of Garvin's clan: Marvin, the younger brother of the deceased leader. Marvin, unlike his brother, did not want to have anything to do with human trafficking, as he feared that he would end up buried six feet under like his brother. Mikalev, on the other hand, had recently become fond of one of the sex 'workers' and was pissed that she wasn't there anymore. Having no information other than that the 'workers' were 'stolen' by Garvin's killers, he blamed it on the new boss, Marvin.

"If this weasel ain't gonna do it, then one of yas better do it— this is the second damn time this has happened to me!" yelled Mikalev, furious. Marvin's surrounding men shifted around nervously, not knowing if they should be scared of Mikalev or Marvin.

"Hell na, sa! Ya see what 'appened t'me bro?" yelled back Marvin. He saw the aftermath, and it sure wasn't pretty. Marvin wanted control of the clan, but also wasn't willing to subject himself to the risks his brother took to stay in power for so long.

Mikalev furiously drank more vodka from his bottle, not sure how they would come up with a solution. Then, Arcus, who was watching from a distance, spoke up.

"Well? Where's the product?"

Marvin slowly turned his head, recognizing the voice. His eyes locked onto Arcus', then he froze, in complete shock and fear.

"U-u-uh, I'm sorry sir, they ain't here... we ain't got no backup either," stuttered Marvin. His men shifted around more nervously, knowing that when Arcus wanted something, he'd get it.

"Then go and get them back *right now*. My man Mik said he wanted one, right?" barked Arcus. He glared at Marvin, who struggled to formulate his next sentence.

"I-I... I c-can't, sa..." Marvin gulped and continued. "D-d-de bounty 'unters are long gone, sa! I ain't 'ave the slightest clue where they s'pose ta be!"

It all happened instantly. What remained of Marvin lay on the floor, split apart from each other;

his head rolled around, completely detached from his remains. A constant stream of blood was flowing out of what presumably was originally his chest, and his organs were splattered across the room. His men rushed to a corner, huddling together in fear.

Mikalev had just witnessed a flash. One second, he was arguing with Marvin; the next, Marvin was a pile of meat jumbled on the floor. He turned around, and saw Arcus licking his blade.

"Ar–Arcus?"

Arcus stopped licking his blade and smiled at Mikalev.

"Good to see you again, Mik."

CHAPTER ? ? - ARCUS' POEM

One by one, they fell from grace,
Into the void, into space.
Looking back, I stayed alive,
But back then - there was no drive.
If I killed one thousand times;
Mik will say that's too much crime.
Not for me, 'twas too little,
My kill count was too fickle.
Further ahead, glory days,
I would conquer, kill and rape.
Now queue the screams, begs, and cries,
I'd spare a laugh when they died.
Morals to me: all but gone,
War, by me, was soon to come.

I'm simply what they are internally. *Humans* are the true savages. They cannot be forgiven for what they've done.

– Arcus Aytfri

CHAPTER 13 – DIARY

———

Villin left for a bounty a day ago. I didn't feel like going, obviously, so I stayed behind. It was quite big, though. She said it was for a "measly" few million. I mean… measly for her meant extreme for anyone else. But it wasn't like she needed the bounty money. I was pretty sure she had more than a trillion dollars in her bank account by now. Perhaps she did the bounties for fun. *There's no way I'd consider bounty hunting fun. Too many interactions required.*

–

Kazjivo had reached the end of the notepad. There

was no more space to write. It had been a long and arduous task, but it felt good to write down his past memories. Reading back through the notepad, he frowned at his earlier self. The earlier memories were embarrassing to him. More times than not, he'd remember how he felt more than what was going on in his surroundings.

He still was socially anxious—but now, he was a bit more confident, more determined to not show it. His mask did a great job at hiding his facial expressions too, making him appear calm and collected at the surface, which also helped.

—

When Villin came back, she seemed cheery as always. The bounty was a simple one; the target actually gave himself up upon seeing her. One of the rare ones where the targets would be captured alive instead of executed on the spot. It was late evening, so she went to take a shower.

Kazjivo was in his room; the guest room for

the condo. His mask was off and he was looking in the mirror. The mask had almost always been on; he couldn't really feel it when it was on, so he usually forgot that he wore it. He raised his hand to touch his face. To think it was molded; crafted by a human. It wasn't natural. *That's why I look… perfect, I guess,* he thought. *No, that's being too vain.* He shook his head, shaking off the thoughts in the process. Yet, he couldn't completely remove the questions about Villin; how she thought of him, if she was attracted to him. He knew there was something there, as she'd often gaze at him longingly, when she thought he wasn't looking.

He stretched his arms, yawned, then laid down on his bed. Everything was calm now, he thought. No more running around hunting criminals. Just living a human's life. What was next? He wasn't sure. He was a machine; a technique machine. In his hands held the power to save or destroy star systems. But what did he want? Kazjivo thought long and hard. He wanted... to be happy.

But what made him happy? Most of the time he had been awake, he was scared or angry. That couldn't be all, he thought. There was always something else inside of him that was there. It wasn't as prominent as his defective emotions, but it was there.

He closed his eyes. He tried to visualize what it was...

—

A figure was moving forward. No matter how fast he tried to run, he couldn't catch up. He tried using his Technique, but it wasn't working. He could only run like a human. He kept running but made no progress. The figure's head slowly turned around while she kept moving forwards. Kazjivo could now see that she was floating; her legs were not moving, yet somehow she was moving ahead faster than him. Her head had now turned 180 degrees around, looking extremely creepy and unnatural. The face was looking backwards. Kazjivo tried to run faster, to see who it was.

"My dear husband, where have you been?"

The face was now clear enough to see—it was… Villin? She spoke again.

"My dear husband… don't you remember me?"

Her smile turned into an impossibly-angled frown. Her mouth grew wider and wider; her sharp teeth—no, canines—now showing. Suddenly, her body snapped back into position with her head, rotating 180 degrees as well. She lowered down into her signature combat position; her metal left hand on her sheath, her right hand on the nodachi's handle. All of this occurred while she was still floating away, as if on an invisible moving platform.

Kazjivo was now out of breath after running for so long. He was bewildered at the ghastly sight in front of him, and unable to speak. Villin's mouth now stretched from ear to ear, her eyes opening up incredibly wide, causing her face to look horrific.

She swung out her blade and pointed it directly at him. Then, she rushed towards him at light speed, plunging the blade directly into his torso.

—

Kazjivo heard a rustling noise. He was awake again, but the nightmare was still fresh in his mind. It clearly wasn't real, but he still felt uneasy. But there was it again—the rustling noise.

Who was in the room? He was tempted to open his eyes, not sure what was there. But he was also pretty tired and hoped it was nothing to worry about so he could go back to sleep. Whatever it was, it was definitely loud enough to wake him up. Maybe… a rat? *We're on the 92nd floor,* he thought, *surely that couldn't happen.* And the condo was clean; there was no food around, either. So it had to be something else.

That was when he noticed a weight on his

torso. He didn't notice at first, but being conscious for a few seconds now, it was very apparent. It felt like someone was sitting on top of him. Perhaps *that* was making the noise. He opened his eyes just by a slit, not moving the rest of his body, unsure of what he would encounter.

It was Villin. She was on top of him, breathing quietly. Her legs were draped over his, locking them in place. Her face was quite close to Kazjivo; her mouth was puckered, as if readying for a kiss. Her right hand was on his stomach, slowly drifting downwards.

Kazjivo's eyes flung wide open. Why was she on him while he was sleeping? Surely she wasn't…

"Villin?" whispered Kazjivo, shocked. Villin's mouth gaped open, then she stumbled back and off of the bed. She put her hands over her mouth, not sure what to do. They could only stare at each other, each processing the situation they were in.

She then left the room and closed the door, leaving Kazjivo stunned.

CHAPTER 14 – VAN HIRE, FOR HIRE

––––

Arcus was now the leader of the remainder of Marvin's gang. He had different ambitions, though. He wasn't interested in petty crime—or even big crime, for that matter. He was going to wreak havoc across the galaxy. To do that, he'd need more minions. On his mind was a certain pirate, one that he'd saved in the past. A certain pirate who commanded a large army of loyal and dangerous members.

–

Van Hire was eating a stale dinner when he got the news. The government of Dos got scared again, and put up a new bounty on his head: $10,000,000,000 this time, ten times the previous one. He sighed. It would take days to get a hold of Arcus. He'd had to fight off bounty hunters in the meanwhile. Then again, Arcus had already wiped off some famous bounty hunters, and people had stopped going after him. Maybe this time around, no hunter would try their luck.

He ordered his new captain to steer the ship to Tamki. He'd end this once and for all—Van Hire decided it was time to kill the leader of Trojan, Lady Angin. He'd always tried to avoid this, as he knew the fight would be very long and bloody. Trojan could also call in other planets from other systems for help. They'd already sent some troops to take him out, which had failed, luckily, but the nerve of them to do so bothered him. But that didn't really annoy him. He was apprehensive for mostly one thing—his brother was part of the government council. Van Hire had never wanted this to come.

—

Van grew up in a small city on the outskirts of

Tamki. His parents were poor farmers, slowly losing business as the years passed by. Pollution and greenhouse farming were making traditional farming obsolete. For most of his childhood, Van worked in the fields on his parent's farm. It was long, gruelling work, and the sun was always beating down on him.

He found solace in going to school. There, the classroom was always cool and he could rest. He spent most of his time in school dozing off, too tired to study. His brother, on the other hand, would study diligently, getting great grades and wowing teachers.

When they were in high school, Van dropped out. He was failing every class and didn't care anymore. He had learned to read, write and count, so in his eyes, high school was just a waste of time.

Van hung out with city gangs, robbed stores, did petty crime. His brother was the polar opposite. He was immaculate, smart, and frowned upon everything Van did. Many times he tried to convince Van out of his criminal ways, but Van would always ignore him.

—

When he turned eighteen, Van got arrested for a bank robbery. He was the only one caught. The police interrogated him, but he refused to snitch on his friends. He was sentenced to six years without parole.

Every month, his brother would visit him and send him money; pity for a brother, if nothing else. When Van entered prison, his brother had just started college. By the time he got out, his brother had finished.

Once out, Van was still like a child and didn't seem to take responsibility seriously. Soon, he was back into his old ways. His brother, on the other hand, got a job at the government and moved out, leaving Van to his own devices.

–

At twenty-five, Van still hadn't accomplished much. The money from his previous robberies were slowly dwindling away. Most of his friends were in prison now, and it would seem like only a matter of time before he would join them again. It was only during another bank robbery did Van find his calling.

–

Van breathed in and out. Since he was doing this solo, it was going to be harder. He was sitting in his car, just outside a large bank. It was evening, and there were fewer people going in and out. He glossed over his plan one more time. *Leave the keys in the car, check. Gun loaded, check. Safety off, check.* He was ready.

Van opened the door and stepped out. He looked around. *Not too many people around,* he thought. *Time to do it.*

Inside the bank, he noticed that there was only one security guard. The guard was looking out the window, clearly bored. There had been no action for months now, and he was getting lax. Van turned his attention to the front. There were a few other patrons in the bank; *not too many,* he thought, *I can handle this.* Still standing by the front entrance, he took the pistol out of his pocket and pointed it at the guard.

—

He didn't expect the police to arrive so fast—he had only just gotten a sack of cash into his car when he heard sirens. He went for the highway and hit the gas, desperate to escape, not worrying about the remaining cash anymore, which laid spread on the bank floor, only a few meters away from the creeping blood of a few resistant victims.

The highway chase was slowly becoming futile for him. His car was running out of hydrogen, and police were everywhere. Thoughts of giving up were bouncing around in his mind. He remembered being in prison. It wasn't that bad. He had friends there, so he'd be alright. But the food was shit and he couldn't hook up with any girls while in there. *Huh,* he thought, *it might really be over for me.* That was when a large truck came into view.

The truck bulldozed past a few police cars and sped up to Van. Van peered through his window, wondering who it could possibly be. Maybe… maybe it was his brother? Obviously not. It was a burly man in a ski mask. He yelled at Van and made a motion with his hand for Van to get on the truck.

Van looked at the rear-view mirrors. The police were gaining on him. He had no choice; either he took this guy's help and perhaps escape, or don't and definitely go back to prison. He opened his windows and stuck his hand out. The man in the truck started yelling something, but his voice was lost in the wind. Van stuck his head outside his car so he could hear what he was saying.

"The money! Throw the money first!" shouted the man. Van looked back. The money was still there, on the passenger side seat. Maybe the guy wanted money for saving him, Van thought. He'd do the same; he'd want money first too. Van reached back and grabbed the bag, then pulled it through the window and gave it to the man in the truck. It was an intricate and risky process, but they got it done. Now, it was Van's turn to escape.

–

Police cruisers turned around and turned off their sirens. The chase was called off—Kugel's gang had interfered, and the police were not willing to risk multiple civilian casualties to risk dealing with his gang.

–

Kugel was the leader of a large and dangerous gang. He saw potential in Van. Van was a risk-taker, and he wasn't scared of doing things alone. Of course, Van would start at the bottom. But his potential showed itself very quickly. Van rose up the ranks rapidly, proving himself to be a natural leader. He was the star of the gang, always willing to risk do-ing things no one else would do. As Van grew in the gang, the gang grew in size. Kugel's gang was soon the largest one in Trojan. They had subsets all over the planet, and would crush smaller gangs to absorb their numbers to boost up their own.

Van soon forgot all about his family; the Kugel gang was his family now. They raided, killed, and raped together. It was only during a raid that Van saw his brother again.

—

It had been years since they'd seen each other. Van had cut ties with his family and was fully embraced by his life of crime. He knew his brother worked in the government, but where and what position, he had no clue.

"V-Van...?"

Van heard a meek voice coming from under a desk. He was in the capital's government building, stealing secret data along with his gang mates. He drew his gun and aimed at whoever was under the desk.

It was his brother, Thor.

Thor was a thin man with a black suit and glasses. He was staring back at Van, scared for his life. All Van could do is stare back, unsure of what to do.

"Hey, Van, let's go! Security's arriving!" shouted a Dossing gang member. They had what they needed, so staying here was no longer necessary.

Van looked at his brother one more time. They were the same, yet so different from each other. Memories of his childhood flooded his mind. He remembered farming in the intense heat, alongside his younger brother. Thor would sometimes take his chores when he was too tired to do them. Thor was a great brother… unlike himself.

Van said nothing, pretending not to recognize Thor. But as he left, a small tear formed in his eye.

–

As time flew by, Van grew more ambitious. He was now Kugel's right-hand man. But he wanted more. He wanted system domination. Kugel was getting old, and barely participated in raids anymore. Kugel was fine with raids and normal crime. Van wasn't.

–

It was just another day when Van entered the mess hall. Kugel was eating lunch with the main crew—a bunch of rough, burly men. They were drinking beer, playing games, and having a good time. Van looked around; all the men here were loyal to Kugel. He glanced back at the doorway to the mess hall. Faces of his men stared back, ready to act whenever Van gave the command.

Van walked until he was behind Kugel, still unnoticed. He then drew his cutlass with one hand, and a pistol with the other. He stabbed Kugel in the back and fired upon the other members of the lunch at the same time. His crew rushed in, mowing down Kugel's loyal. With them gone, Van could start his plan of ruling all of Dos.

—

Arcus descended on Van Hire's captain ship in an instant. One moment everything was normal; the next moment it was cut in half. The humans on board, not being able to withstand outer space, died quickly.

Van Hire was dying. He was floating in space; all was quiet. Debris from his ship floated around him; he could barely see anything, as he was losing his sight fast.

A white figure appeared in front of him. He racked his brain for answers; he tried to remember who it was. His brain was losing its power very quickly. He struggled more… and more… he was fading away.

Just before he died, a name came to Van Hire's mind—*Arcus!*

—

Now Arcus had an army. But they were thugs, miscreants. They could kill civilians, but how would they fare against a real army? He looked at his men and tried to find good candidates; someone that he could rely on. There were a few decent ones, those that were stronger than the rest. But none were of top-notch quality to Arcus. What he needed was someone of a better breed; a higher caliber.

Arcus paced around his desk, planning his next move. He had enough men now. It wouldn't really matter if they died; he could get more. He could send wave after wave of them to attack, and if they rebelled, he'd kill them. Of course, he would waste his time on them if that happened, but he was willing to take the risk.

Mikalev peeked his head through the open door. Arcus looked up and frowned.

"What is it, Mik?" said Arcus. His thoughts were now jumbled up.

Mikalev sauntered in casually. "Well, ya need a good man, right? Just look at bounties, and find 'em!" said Mikalev, impressed with his own idea.

Arcus thought about it for a second. Actually, it was a genius idea. Just find whoever had the largest bounty and recruit them. Van Hire was the highest; but now that he was dead, it went to a guy named Vandl. He was a gang leader in Sol star system. Sol system was very advanced and had powerful armies, but somehow Vandl managed to keep his gang large and persistent throughout the system. Vandl's gang specialized in drug and arms trades; he'd definitely had the firepower Arcus' army needed.

"Mikalev, find Vandl for me. Leave him alive, now. He's no use to me dead," ordered Arcus. Mikalev saluted, then rushed out of the room. His plan was now set in motion—as long as his nemesis didn't come after him, it'd be easy tidings. The first target on his mind was the closest one: Trojan of Dos.

—

Mangled bodies littered the floor of the government building, painting the once-white floor red. Soldiers, civilians, politicians—none were spared. A loud siren was wailing in the background, falling on the ears of the dead, who could no longer take heed.

Arcus had ordered his army to attack Trojan earlier today. While they prepared the attack, Arcus flew down and started destroying the city of Tamki by himself. He wanted to savour the fun before his army came. By the time his army arrived, Tamki was in ruins. He ordered his strike force to kill the survivors—women and children included. The rest of his army was ordered to attack other major cities around the planet. They would weaken them—so when Arcus arrived, he would clean up the remainder quickly.

"Y-you... why?"

Arcus heard a meek voice. He turned around, and saw a skinny man in a suit and wearing glasses. The man was shielded from Arcus' blade by his fellow council members; he was injured, but still alive.

Arcus scrunched his face. The man looked familiar, he thought. Why was that so? As Arcus walked closer to him, he made the connection. The government man looked like Van Hire, but a lot skinnier and cleaner-shaven.

"Do you know a 'Van Hire'?" asked Arcus. The skinny man shivered as he replied.

"Y-yes, that's my brother. A-are you part of his clan?"

Arcus frowned. Was he part of Van Hire's clan? No, Van Hire's clan was now part of *his* army. This man implied Arcus was weak enough to actually be under Van Hire's command. Well, thought Arcus, he can join his brother's *clan* in the grave.

Arcus thrust his greatsword into the man,

the forward blade piercing the chest, the rear blade crushing the head. Blood poured out of the massive holes as the man's body fell to the ground. Arcus spat at the dead body in disgust. No one who disrespected Arcus lived long.

No one.

CHAPTER 15 – MEMORY

———

Kazjivo and Villin were preparing to leave Ceti. A new 'mega' bounty was just issued in Sol system, and Villin wanted to go there to hunt. It wasn't that she needed the money. She enjoyed the thrill of the hunt; the thrill of demolishing opponents in battle, the feeling of awe when she turned in the bounties, the clamouring of fans who recognized her.

Kazjivo, on the other hand, was deep in his thoughts, uninterested in the bounty. The events of last night were still on his mind. In the morning, Villin spoke to him like nothing happened. They went about their daily duties like this. Kazjivo, not sure what to do, stayed quiet for the most part, not daring to bring the subject up. The silence was weighing heavily on Villin, but she did not show it outwardly at all. She tried to lighten up the mood and give him a prod in the back, if he was too quiet for too long. But he remained listless, still troubled by her lack of acknowledgement, and his own anxiety.

—

There were headed to Nades, in Sol system. Villin acquired the bounty online, as the bounty giver was on Earth. They had advanced enough technology that one could do so in space, millions of kilometers away from the planet. The target in question was named Vandl. He was the leader of a dangerous gang that plagued Sol system. The bounty was the largest one available in the galaxy after Van Hire— it was for $900,000,000. It was an impossibly dangerous bounty for the normal hunter. But for Villin? It would probably be easy for her.

She sat in the front seat by the steering controls. Kazjivo stood by the rear entranceway, wondering if he should come in. The ominous atmosphere that had been persisting throughout the day had continued, and they'd yet to talk since they got on the ship.

It could have been chance, but a certain memory came to mind. It was when he was learning to use his Technique. He was swinging his greatsword in that empty room, trying his hardest to control the higher dimension. Villin came into the room and told him that to use his Technique, he needed to think of what his purpose was.

He remembered what he thought of that day. At first, he thought of nothing—he wasn't sure what he was supposed to do. What he *could* do. After all, he was defective. He hated his defects, his fears. The anxiety that he felt when he saw strangers. But that wasn't what helped him use his Technique. It was only when his meaning came to him that he was able to control the higher dimen-

sion. It manifested as an image, one he clearly remembered; only then, did he feel a surge of energy,
was he able to manipulate the higher dimension.

The memory flooded back into his mind;
the visions and sounds, clear as day.

Who am I...

Who is coming?

Then, the door opened. A stunning person
had opened the door, and he had to glance away momentarily. She was simply too beautiful to look at,
so much so that his anxiety forced him to look
away. But he slowly turned his head and looked at
the stranger—he had to know who she was. As he
gazed at her beautiful, violetish-blue eyes, she noticed him, and her eyes stared straight back at him,
piercing his soul.

—

He had always known that since the moment he met
her, he was in love. But how would he ever approach her? The position he was at—the one she'd

given him—felt content. It was alright, fine. She was married to him too; it was just that he had no memories. She took care of him due to their past. But what was he now? How did his past self marry her? He was frustrated. If he did it before, that means he could do it now, right?

Kazjivo second-guessed himself. Perhaps he wasn't at the stage yet—the part that he was in the past, when he got into a relationship with Villin. He definitely didn't feel ready. Inside, he was still scared. He might act more confident now, but his mind was still constantly anxious.

But Villin *did* want something more. The night that she was on top of him... after all, to her, nothing had really changed other than his memories. Even if he remembered nothing, to her, he looked like the same man that she fell in love with. He *was* the same man. Maybe she wanted to believe that nothing had happened; that Kazjivo would remember her, and that everything would be back to normal.

The double engines of Argua rumbled in the distance. Other than that, all was quiet.

–

Kazjivo stepped forward. He was headed towards her.

Clop…

Clop…

Clop.

It was the same sound that he had first heard, after he woke up for the first time. The sound of Villin's boots, slowly approaching the room he was in. Only this time, it was his.

Kazjivo ignored everything going on in his mind. *Don't think, just act*, he told himself. He took a step forward, then another one, then another one. Villin was getting closer as he walked forward. Her golden hair glistened, reflecting the light of the stars. It was long and soft; it was perfect hair, for the perfect being.

Kazjivo wrapped his arms around Villin's neck. He was scared of her reaction, but held firm nonetheless. Villin didn't move for what seemed to be the longest moment. She then slowly lifted her right hand and placed it on top of his arm, holding it steady.

CHAPTER 16 – ENEMIES ONCE MORE

———

Nades was far away from its star, Sol. Almost no light from Sol reached it—so how was there civilization here, you might ask? Well, valuable resources begets a booming economy. And where there's money to be made, mankind will leap at the chance to acquire all of it. The unassuming Nades was the holy grail of resources. It had tons of chromiq-carbon; the strongest material in the universe. It also had other precious metals—diamonds, gold, platinum, chrome, carbon—in abundance. It was a hard place to live, that's true. But, if you were rich, this place only sought to make you richer. It was the civilization on Eviel that first settled here. The main population nearby were the humans from Earth. They ignored Nades, as it was extremely far and devoid of life. They had assumed it was a barren planet that was always cold. Barren it was; cold as well. But resources they had, and the Terrans missed out on their opportunity.

Eviel had grown rich and powerful from their mining of Nades. They had long conquered the entire planet before others had found out, and so blocked out any other planets from getting land. This monopoly saw Eviel's rapid technological advancements.

With Eviel gone, and the owners of Nades' land with it, Terrans and Volkelings quickly descended upon the planet, securing as much territory as possible. One such Terran was named Vandl. He was a powerful mercenary who quickly rallied up an army to secure territory. As there wasn't any law enforcement on Nades, he and his army killed nearby landowners. As Vandl grew rich, his army grew in size. As hard as it was to live on Nades, they certainly had the resources to keep going. Money was no problem. Vandl created powerful weapons built from rare metals, and special drugs unique to Nades. Controlling the largest majority of Nades, Vandl was becoming a king in his own right.

But with power and resources, come other beings, desperate for the power Vandl held. Vandl, being a seasoned warrior, knew this was bound to come. He trained his men to be elite warriors. Many tried to dethrone Vandl, but none succeeded. And so, Vandl became the greatest kingpin in all of Sol system.

–

Kazjivo looked around him. Nades was a dark place, lit up mostly by the large lamps that dotted the streets, ever so regularly. The city they were in, called Naberus, was the capital of the country. Somewhere here was Vandl—the ruler of Nade, the largest country in Nades. Kazjivo assumed that

Vandl knew of the bounty on his head. There should've been more guards around, and all Kazjivo saw were civilians and workers milling about. Vandl wasn't dumb, though. *Perhaps it seems this way so the unaware bounty hunter would be overconfident,* thought Kazjivo.

Up ahead was the main government building. It was a long building, coloured a dark grey, blocky, with small windows dotting the perimeter. Two guards stood in front of the building, both heavily armed. As Kazjivo and Villin walked up to the entrance, the two guards crossed their guns and blocked their path.

"You must be new here. One does not simply enter the king's castle," said a guard. He continued his warning. "Permission must be granted ahead of time. Only one person has reserved a meeting, and he's already inside."

Villin had a slight frown on her face. She was figuring out the best approach here, one that would incorporate stealth, not destruction. She asked the guard, "How may I reserve a meeting, if you will be so kind?"

"You must call at least twenty-four hours before your desired time. If you make a call now, there is a good chance you can see the king tomorrow," suggested the guard. Kazjivo looked at Villin, not sure what she would do. Villin's frown grew deeper.

"I want to go in now. If there's only one person meeting the king right now, surely he has extra time?" prodded Villin. She was pressuring them, seeing how they would react.

"The king's time is very important. Just so you know, missy, common rabble ain't entitled to the king's time," sneered the guard. The other guard made a slightly audible chuckle. They were thoroughly enjoying their authority; they didn't get to enjoy it for too long, however.

Villin went into her combat stance, then cut

both the guards in half—within a split second. The top halves of their bodies slid off and landed on the ground with a dull *thud*. Villin then looked at Kazjivo, as if nothing had happened. She stated, "I think the guards changed their minds. Let's go."

The inside of the building was tall, vast, and filled with paintings from top to bottom—all stolen from famous museums. Kazjivo didn't have much time to admire it, however, as Villin pulled him along to where the king's chamber was located. While walking to their location, Kazjivo couldn't help but notice that there were no guards around. It seemed weird to have none as backup. If the two guards at the entrance were killed, shouldn't there be more to protect the king?

Two massive doors were in their way. The king's chamber was behind the doors. If it was locked, they'd have to break it open. But it wasn't— the door was left slightly ajar, as if someone had already entered. Kazjivo looked at Villin, who shrugged. It was probably left open by the previous visitor. Villin led the way, and they entered the chamber.

—

"Well? Ya join or not, ya choice," growled Mikalev. He then spoke in a more demeaning tone. "Or ya can die, s'no problem to me, I 'sure ya. It'll be bad news for Arc, yea, but we'll get a massive paycheck fer the bounty. Ain't bad—that's a lot of money. Well? Speak up!"

Vandl was sitting on his bed, paralyzed in fear. He had a gigantic axe head pointed at him. All of his guards had just been slaughtered like they were nothing. Whoever this man was, he was extremely dangerous.

Knowing the only choice he had was to surrender, he sighed. "Okay, just spare the rest of my men, there's no need to kill any more," said Vandl, head hung low. Mikalev smiled.

"Thanks to your cooperation, Vandl, I won't

have ta kill any more of yer fleshies. A wise choice, if I do say so ma-self," said Mikalev. This was too easy for him. A dangerous kingpin? To Mikalev, that was nothing. The entire base was a cakewalk. He set up a fake meeting and breezed through the front guards. Once he reached the chamber, he killed all the guards inside the building. Vandl and his gang stood no chance.

"Mikalev... what are you doing here?" sputtered Villin. Mikalev spun around, surprised by her voice. He saw Villin and Kazjivo standing at the doorway, their weapons drawn and at the ready.

"Eh, what are yas doing 'ere? Wait... this un 'ere is mines, I got him first!" Mikalev shouted. The situation had turned sour very quickly. If Villin wanted the bounty on Vandl, she'd probably fight him for it. Mikalev knew he would probably lose in that fight, as her Technique control was unmatched.

"Don't tell me you're working with Arcus again? I thought you changed," said Villin.

Kazjivo's hands trembled as he held his blade. If a fight broke out, he'd have to react fast.

"Eh… none of ya business, Villi. I do what I want," spat Mikalev. He was looking around rapidly, searching for a place to escape. Even if Arcus would be angry, he was worried about the here and now. And right now his life was in danger.

"The bounty is mine, Mik. I'm sure Arcus will understand," pressured Villin. She didn't want to fight Mikalev, but if he really was working with Arcus, then he was up to no good.

Mikalev had to leave now. He looked up; the ceiling would do the trick.

"Well then. Bye-bye, Villi. Hope ya ain't gonna interrupt any more of our operations, I wouldn't want ya ta get hurt, now." With his warning said, Mikalev flew upwards, smashed through the roof, and out of the castle.

Now, all that was left of Mikalev's presence was the giant hole in the ceiling and the piles of dead guards littered on the marbled chamber floor. Villin turned her focus back to Vandl. Vandl stared back at Villin. Now was his chance—he could grab his gun and fend off these bounty hunters. Vandl threw off his blankets and ran for his rifle. Villin, seeing him run, scarcely missed a beat as she charged at him.

Vandl's body split into three pieces and splattered onto the wall. Villin spun her blade around multiple times, flinging off Vandl's blood, then slowly sheathed it. The mighty kingpin, Vandl, was now dead.

CHAPTER 17 — A CITY IN RUINS

Arcus paced around the roof of the skyscraper he was standing on. The news of Villin shocked him. He had thought she would've secluded herself from society forever, hiding from him; but apparently, this was not so. Mikalev also had seen Kazjivo; that he was alive, that he seemed to follow Villin. So that was why Villin was so brazen now; she had *him* to protect her. Arcus was sure he'd never wake up. He had used all his Technique on *that* attack. He was the only one that could use it, as he was the only one with a maximum power rating. While his Technique control wasn't as good as Villin's, he was still the only one that could blow apart a planet in one hit. But Mikalev did say Kazjivo didn't talk at all and seemed only a shell of a machine. Maybe he wasn't going to be much of a threat.

The two were there for a bounty, not for Vandl's men, nor Nades, for that matter. They were technique machines, just like him; they were the same kind. It was possible they wouldn't interfere with his plans, right? Also, Villin wouldn't risk getting killed just to stop Arcus again. Not this time— not when Arcus was fully healed. Arcus needed her to stay out of this; he needed all his power for his current plans.

Yes, his plans. Arcus looked around from where he stood. He was on the only skyscraper left standing in Tamki. The rest of the city was completely destroyed. The survivors were being butchered by his army; those who refused to do so were sliced up and shown to everyone else as an ex-ample, including that pesky Lady Angin.

She'd mouthed off to him in her final moments and her mangled body was to be specially displayed to the public as a warning. The rest of Trojan was slowly but surely being conquered. An entire planet, demolished in a few days—and this time, Arcus didn't have drain any Technique. He smiled. More planets would fall, more civilizations destroyed. The Milky Way galaxy was soon to be his. *Soon,* he thought, *they'll be enslaved. Just as my kind had once been—hate is a beautiful seed, and it shall grow into a beautiful blossom of death.*

–

Kazjivo and Villin were on Earth, reaping the rewards of the bounty. News had already spread across the system that Vandl was killed. They weren't noticed when they first landed, but as they walked through a busy plaza, they started to get recognized, and people pointed at them. Kazjivo immediately felt the gazes on him. Looking around, people were gawking at them, as if they were famous celebrities. He glanced at Villin, who seemed to ignore it all.

"Villin, people are staring at us. I don't really like this," said Kazjivo. He stood straight and seemed to ignore it on the outside, but inside, his body was going numb.

"Ignore them. I've been recognized a lot lately—they're looking at me, not you."

Villin looked back at Kazjivo. He was uncomfortable, but it was hard to tell at a first glance. Looking closer, though, she could tell his balance was starting to get a bit wonky, signs of the stress the situation was causing. She held her right hand a bit back for him. Kazjivo saw this and latched on, slightly comforted.

—

Arcus was on his spaceship, sipping some coffee. As far as the eye could see, from his vantage point, it all was his. Planet Trojan had fallen, and with it, the civilization there. He would keep a few alive for slave labour. They would salvage the remains of

Trojan and build a new civilization that worshipped him.

The fleshy humans were weak. He may have been modelled after them, but he was superior. He was a god compared to them.

–

News of Trojan's demise spread rapidly. It caused terrible panic on every star system; fears of another Eviel incident began to spread. A single video recording, which had captured the events, soon became viral. It was taken on Tamki; it showed a flying man in white destroying the city. He flew at incredible speeds, cutting through multiple buildings with each swing. He was not human; his feats were impossible. It was the machine who had destroyed Eviel; it was the Evil Dressed In White, Arcus.

Armies across the galaxy mobilized to defend their planets. They were all worried—who wouldn't be, after seeing the aftermath of Eviel? And now, Trojan was basically gone as well. They knew about Arcus. But he had rarely shown himself after that incident, making it seem like he had all but stayed in the shadows. But the video was clear as day; an army had taken over the planet, led by Arcus himself.

Now all the planets in the galactic alliance could only wonder—who would be next?

–

The leaders of the galactic alliance all joined together a day after the news. They had travelled as fast as possible from all around the galaxy to reconvene at Volke. Their planets could be the next target, and so they all conjured a special response plan. The moment that a planet was under attack, they'd send a distress call out to everyone else. Then, the entire galaxy's armies would converge on that one planet.

But even with a solid plan in action, they were scared. Arcus hadn't just destroyed any planet —he had destroyed *Eviel* all those years ago. If the most advanced civilization had lost to this man, who were they to think they could stop him?

—

"Silence! Silence!" shouted out Sir Ramus, pounding the roundtable with his fist. The other members' voices slowly died down as they focused their attention on the Volkean leader.

"We may have made a mistake about Trojan. It wasn't Van Hire who was the problem, it was Arcus Aytfri. Perhaps we should have assisted Lady Angin…" He drifted off mid-sentence, possibly regretful of the last time they met.

"Who helped her put a bounty up? None of you did. You all did fudge all to help," sputtered out Sir York. He was close to Lady Angin, and was the one who put up the majority of the sum for Van Hire. Sir Ramus, not one to lose control of the conversation, countered.

"If I recall, Sir York, when you had a chance to defend her, you stayed silent, like the rest of us." The other members nodded their heads in agreement, recalling that day. Sir York had only decided to follow Lady Angin after she had left.

Sir York turned red, flustered, unsure how to respond. He was usually quiet, and was definitely afraid to speak his mind at that time. The feelings of regret filled him, as a different outcome might have occurred had he spoken up.

"No matter, no matter. That is behind us now. We must face Mr. Aytfri now. The largest bounty ever must be placed on him. We will all have to chip in. The amount sufficient is, I believe... one sextillion dollars."

Gasps filled the room. Did that much money even exist in the universe, let alone a single galaxy? As the table chatter grew louder, Sir Ramus hushed them down to continue.

"Obviously, no one can defeat Mr. Aytfri by themselves. And no one is able to collect that bounty. It's simply there to show the public how dangerous he is. We must gather all our forces and fight him as a joint force. A galactic force, if you will, billions strong. Mr. Aytfri is a threat to every planet. If we do not stop him now, extinction is almost certain."

The alliance members looked at each other and nodded in agreement. Eviel was destroyed, Trojan had fallen. They didn't want their own planets to be next. While before, they could ignore the looming threat, as Arcus wasn't actively attacking planets, now they had no choice. They would all have to pitch in, together, in an attempt to stop the avenging machine.

Sir Ramus, seeing the nods, saw that as agreement. He said, "I see we all can agree. I expect half of your planet's forces to sign up for the defence force, no less. It must be massive. It should be decisive. It *will* be successful."

The final measure was put in place. If all hope seemed to be lost on a planet, they'd nuke it with everything they had. Millions of nukes would rain down on the planet, wiping out the entire population; and with it, Arcus and his army. It would be the last ditch effort; the ultimate lesser of two evils.

Multiple strike forces were called to action. They didn't know if they would succeed, but they had to try. Whoever joined would do it for all of mankind. There was no guarantee of survival.

–

Just after cashing in the bounty of Vandl, news broke out of the takeover of Trojan. Kazjivo and Villin had walked over to a high bridge overlooking the city square. Millions of people were there, waiting to hear the alliance's answer to Arcus. Soon, an official came onto the city square's high stage and gave a speech about what happened. Most of the crowd already knew what had happened, but it was still terrifying to hear it from an official nonetheless. Kazjivo had never seen him, but he recognized the description. A flying man, destroying a city, dressed in white; there was no doubt in Kazjivo's mind. He had tuned out of the speech for quite a while, disappearing into his thoughts. Thinking about what conversations he had with Arcus before. If he was like a brother to him in the past. Then he shook his head. He should be listening; the galaxy; no, the universe, was in jeopardy.

"...the decision was to send a joint strike force to Trojan and hopefully eliminate Arcus' army. Our strike force is a massive contingent, consisting of millions of the best and brightest from each planet. They are the alliance's best men and women. They will be equipped to the bone—so fear not, citizens of Earth and beyond, I assure you that they will succeed. Be it days, months, or years; we'll avenge the people of Trojan and Eviel."

Some in the crowd cheered, blissfully unaware of the extent of Arcus' power. Kazjivo looked over to Villin, gauging her reaction. Her face did not move; she seemed unaffected by speech. She turned to look at Kazjivo, and noticed he was looking at her.

"They'll all die. They have nukes, yes—but it'll do nothing to Arcus. What they need to do is figure out how to reason with him. Only then will they have a sliver of a chance to survive," said Villin, plainly. Kazjivo was a bit confused with her wording—were they not going to stop him?

"We aren't going to stop Arcus and his plan for galactic domination?" questioned Kazjivo. He had always thought Villin would be on the side of humans. She had helped them so many times, from bounty hunting dangerous criminals to her planetary donations. It didn't seem like she hated them.

"Well, do you want to?" asked Villin. Kazjivo was stunned.

"I mean, I think we have to," he said. He got that they weren't machines like him and Villin; but they were their creators, they were modelled after them.

"We don't have to. There's no reason to, anyway. They're just flesh... they're unimportant. They created us as *slaves* to do their bidding." Villin paused, looking back out to the massive crowd beneath them, then continued.

"I shall never be loyal to them. If Arcus wishes to kill them all, who am I to rid him of his desire?"

She kept her gaze forward, staring blankly into nothingness, her face devoid of emotion.

Kazjivo shook his head. This was not like the Villin he knew, the kind and caring Villin who was always there for him. He spoke up, emphatic-ally.

"Ever since I woke up, we've not been treated wrongly, right? They look at us like we're just another human. A lot of them admire you, Vill. You're famous—they know you as the best bounty hunter in the universe. They might not know we're machines yet. But if we help them, we machines will be the heroes, not the villains."

Villin gazed intently at the crowd below. Millions of humans were there; they all had their own lives, they all had families, and they all wanted to live. They were sentient, the very flesh and bone the technique machines were based on. Now, if ever, would be the time to step up and do what they were created to do—protect humankind.

Villin turned back to Kazjivo, and whispered softly.

"I am a villain, Kaz."

CHAPTER 18 – WAR

─────

Sol system had Nades; the planet of resources.
But it was now under control by Arcus. With control
of Nades, he would be able to build larger and more
powerful ships there. He didn't have Vandl, since
the poor S.O.B. was killed by Villin, but it didn't
matter anyway. He'd just go there himself, kill any
resistance remaining, then force everyone there to
work for him. Earth was a juicy target too. With
Eviel gone, it was now the most advanced planet in
the galaxy. It would be a great place to set up a main
base. Trojan was pretty much destroyed already, and
the technology there was quite dated anyway. It
wouldn't be too hard for Arcus to take Earth—just

kill all who resisted, then enslave the survivors.

—

Captain Jeremy was leading his assault squad. He was only one of the million space fighters that were flying towards Trojan. Each pilot had the same mission—to nuke Trojan. On his spacecraft were two nuclear missiles, one under each wing. They had to destroy what was left of Trojan, hopefully wiping out Arcus and his army as well as his re-supply chain, before he could ruin another planet. Jeremy felt sorry for the innocents still left on Trojan, but this was for the greater good. Trojan was a lost cause already. Now, he had to worry about his own planet—Earth.

"Unit 4089, ready warheads."

Jeremy spoke loudly and confidently to his squadron. Trojan was very close now, but it was nothing like he remembered. Now it had a dark haze surrounding the planet, and there were no lights to be seen coming from the surface, indicating most of its electric infrastructure was destroyed.

Jeremy knew some people from Trojan. He hoped they had survived; but realistically, they were probably dead. He shook his head. Now was not the time to reminisce about days long gone. Now was the time to save the universe.

—

Mikalev looked to the sky. He squinted his eyes, looking into Dos. Something was there, but he couldn't quite make it out. Dos' light was too bright, blocking sight of whatever was there. Intrigued, he moved his way further up the atmosphere.

Closing in on Trojan was a massive swarm of space fighters. They were going towards the planet at their maximum speed. It didn't look too fast from Mikalev's point of view, but he knew they would arrive soon enough. He rushed back to the last standing skyscraper of Tamki, to speak with Arcus.

"Eh, Arc, there's a big group of fighters

com'n here, should we stop 'em?"

"Ah, they've arrived. Humans are so very predictable."

—

Jeremy had his finger on the missile trigger. Any moment now, and the general would give the order to fire. They had to get close enough to get an accurate shot off, as the missiles were dumb, to avoid getting spoofed by flares or anti-radar tech. It was all point, fire, then retreat. He looked to his side window. He saw his squadron mates flying alongside him. He felt more confident in himself. *You're the captain, Jeremy.* He thought to himself. *If they're doing this, so can you.*

The light of Dos gave the spacecraft visible shadows, even this far out from the star. The planet Trojan, which was relatively nearby, had a strange atmosphere about it; surrounding it was a yellowish haze. Was that dust from the ring, or smoke from the flames on the surface? Jeremy clutched his steering stick tighter. *Any time now, Jeremy. It'll be over soon, and you can go back to your family.* Jeremy quietly recited a verse from the holy Axudo. The order was expected to come any moment now.

–

Arcus looked at the giant space force headed towards his planet. The overall size was quite large, but he had destroyed larger, recalling Eviel. As he concentrated his Technique, white light started to coat his weapon. Mikalev floated nearby, watching Arcus. He was going to do it again, but on a smaller scale. Just enough to wipe out this… well, alliance thing.

–

Before Jeremy got the order to fire, his spaceship was incinerated. He never saw what killed him.

–

"I'm impressed," mused Mikalev. Arcus had just cleaned up everything in front of them. There were a billion spacecraft in front of them a few seconds ago; now, there was nothing. Arcus swung his arms around, excited.

"That was easy. I could do that all day," said Arcus. Obviously, it wasn't the same as blowing up an entire planet, but it was a great feat nonetheless. Now the alliance would know his power. This task force was equipped with the best technology they had to offer—and they didn't even last a second. Who knows how large a percentage they were, too. It had to be a sizable portion of the alliance's overall fleet, based on numbers alone. *Any more to come would be ill-equipped as well,* he thought. *They had sent out their best in an attempt to end me in one strike. In one move, they've already lost.*

Arcus' next move was to go to Nades. He planned to do three moves at once. He would go to Nades, alone, and clear it out. Mikalev would lead the majority of his troops to Mars and take over it; all the while a newly appointed captain Harris (a

$1,000,000 bounty target from KJ4) would lead the rest of the troops to Earth, effectively stopping the humans from saving Mars. Whether or not Harris' troops would survive was irrelevant, as by the time they bled out, Arcus and Mikalev would've cleared their planets and be ready to engage Earth.

—

Unbeknownst to Arcus, a familiar face was on the Terran planet. The man polished his blade for the tenth time. He looked at his reflection on his blade. It was clear, yet he put it down and resumed polishing it. He shivered, even though he wasn't cold. It was from the knowledge of what was to come. He knew Arcus was coming; he knew his planet was next. How he would win, he did not know. But he would try to the best of his ability.

He may have failed Eviel, but he refused to fail Earth.

CHAPTER 19 – LED TO THE SLAUGHTER

———

"I am a villain, Kaz." Villin had a blank look in her eyes. She stared right into Kazjivo, emotionless. Kazjivo didn't hesitate—he stepped towards her and gave her a hug. He didn't let go. He didn't want to let go.

"You aren't a villain. Trust me."

Villin stayed in his embrace—but deep down, she knew that wasn't true. After all, she had lied to him this entire time.

–

Captain Harris looked at Earth. It was a beautiful planet, full of colour. *Too bad it was going to get destroyed*, he thought. With Arcus on his side, they could conquer planets with ease. It was crazy to him at the start; did this guy really have superpowers? But it became apparent very quickly, that yes, he did have superpowers—and more.

Harris' team's mission was to go directly for the government tower in Bastea. He had around a hundred thousand troops; a rough group filled with vagabonds and thugs, yes, but a hundred thousand nonetheless. The plan was to get in there, kill Sir York, and hopefully control the capital until Mikalev's forces arrived for the knockout blow.

–

On the ground, Earth was preparing for the invasion. Thousands of fighter pilots were sent out to intercept the incoming troops. All civilian space travel was suspended, as expected. The leaders of Earth were expecting to use some nukes above the atmosphere; they could only use them there. If the enemy made it into the atmosphere, they would be at risk from their own nukes. They'd have to fight man to man, which could turn ugly very fast.

Mars was requesting help, but Earth could not oblige. They had their hands full on their own defense; Mars would have to wait for the alliance's troops to arrive. In the meantime, they'd have to fend for themselves.

—

Mikalev looked around the city he was in. Many buildings were toppled over. Fires raged all over the place, burning the city. *Mars was too easy,* he thought. Their army was woefully unprepared for such an invasion. The Martians had relied on Ter-rans, to their own detriment, as they never came. Mars' naturally small army, combined with their blissfully unaware sense of security, was what made this all easier. The people of Mars never expected that *they* would be attacked. Obviously, Arcus would go after big targets like Ceti, Volke, or Earth... right? But Mars?

Yes, thought Mikalev. *Definitely Mars.* It

was a good launching point into Earth. It also served as a barrier from the alliance. Now they could station troops here and fend off the alliance while Earth was being ravaged.

—

Nades was a dismal place. The people gave up instantly, sure, but it was always dark and had no natural air, so people had to walk around in their space clothing, making communication difficult for them. Arcus was disgusted—this planet was hideous to him, an ugly mining wasteland best left to his underlings. No matter; he instructed his newly acquired bounty targets to act as Nades' command. Their goal was to build more weapons, armour, and ships for future invasions on other planets. Once done, he quickly headed back to Mars, where he was expecting good news.

—

Kazjivo and Villin walked into the highrise, escorted by armed guards. Hearing the door open, the old man sitting at the large table which adorned the government room turned to face them. He clasped his hands together, leaning his head forward to get a better view. Yes, he recognized one of them. That was the legendary bounty hunter: Villin.

He motioned his guards to leave before starting. "Welcome to my humble building, you two. I am Sir York, leader of Sol star system. As I'm sure you're aware, we are in a great crisis at this moment, and I do believe I will need your help."

Villin's eyes flitted around the room warily, but otherwise seemed uninterested. Sir York, attempting to break the ice, asked a question. "Esteemed Lady Villin, may I ask who is with you?"

She answered, curtly. "Kazjivo."

Sir York chuckled awkwardly, unsure of who the man was supposed to be. Well, it didn't matter. Probably just her personal bodyguard or something to that effect. In any case, he didn't exactly have too much time to waste.

"I am most surprised that you've responded to our call for help, Lady Villin, as you've never responded before. But I'm sure you're aware of the predicament we're in…" droned on Sir York, before he was interrupted.

"Get on with it. What do you want us to do?" spoke Villin, sharply.

"Ah, yes, we need you to intercept Mr. Aytfri's advance force. The galactic alliance reinforcements will take a while to arrive, and for now, you may be Earth's only hope," said Sir York. He had asked for reinforcements, but after the strike force was annihilated at Trojan, other planetary leaders were scared for their own planet's safety and were shoring up their own defenses rather than contributing to the second strike force. His last resort was to attempt to contact the legendary bounty hunter, Villin. However, she had never responded to anyone in the past; she would do whatever she wanted, in her own time frame, her own way. It was a pleasant surprise when the call came in that she'd meet him. Well, if there was any time to finally get in contact, it was definitely this time, when the fate of Earth lay in peril.

Villin nodded, then turned around, leaving. The tall man beside her followed her. Even now, she remained ever so enigmatic.

Sir York sighed, turning his chair back to the window. Outside was a beautiful view of Bastea. A dazzling city filled with millions of people, vibrant and full of life. To think that it might never be the same in the coming days. *Man has a soul. Machines, created by our hands, do not,* thought Sir York. *Those soulless robots will not prevail. Not while I live, by the grace of the holy Axudo!*

—

The first sirens went off in the morning. Kazjivo and Villin looked at the news, and it was the worst-case scenario—Arcus' troops had entered Earth at night and were engaged in multiple battles above Bastea. Kazjivo had formulated a plan. They would launch up towards the battle with their ship, then exit their ship and eliminate Arcus' troops.

Villin had painted a large blue cross on Argua, much to its dismay, to let others know it was friendly to Earth. As they came closer to the battle, they could see ships engaged in combat. Some were on fire, while others were falling to the ground, either destroyed or being flown to their demise by an incapacitated pilot.

Once a few kilometers high, and in the thick of the battle, it was time to go.

"Argua. Roof hatch," barked out Villin.

The yellow glob appeared, coming out of the control screen, then spun around before replying.

"Yes ma'am, the hatch is opening now!"

The hatch opened inwards, the passing wind blowing loudly into the main cabin. Villin went out first, then beckoned for Kazjivo. Looking up, it was a mess. The sky was dark with explosive powder. Screams of missiles and gunfire were a constant assault on the ears, loud enough to deafen a human. Villin put her hand on Kazjivo's shoulder, reassuring him. It was time to fight.

—

Kazjivo slashed down an intruding ship with one cut of his double-bladed greatsword. Then, he would fly to the next and cut that one down. No matter how fast he went, though, there were always more ships to cut down. It seemed like there was an endless supply. During combat, he would look at Villin and see her progress. Her incredibly long blade was extended kilometers into the sky, clearing swaths of enemies with each swipe.

—

"KAZJIVO, KAZJIVO..." rumbled a loud, deafening voice.

Kazjivo turned around, not recognizing it. It

came from the ship; Argua. This must've been its outdoor voice.

"THERE IS A FLYING OBJECT OUT THERE MOVING JUST LIKE YOU. I'M NOT SURE IF YOU SHOULD BE WORRIED ABOUT IT, BUT IN CASE IT'S ARCUS, I THOUGHT YOU SHOULD KNOW."

Kazjivo, ears still ringing in pain, received the updated information about the unknown flying object. It was a few kilometers west; he nodded to the ship, then flew towards his new heading.

Kazjivo dashed at max speed, knowing if Arcus saw Villin, he'd definitely try to finish what he wasn't able to finish five years ago. Kazjivo would need to intercept him—before Villin got hurt.

Kazjivo then saw a red streak that was zipping around in the distance. It seemed to move nearly as fast as he did, and it was blowing up ships as well. Looking around, there weren't many ships close by; it must've destroyed them in this area. He flew towards the red figure, unsure of what it was, but curious to find out. As he got closer, the red figure finally noticed him. It turned around, then rushed Kazjivo.

Their blades met with a loud clang. Kazjivo parried the attacks with ease, undeterred. He looked closer at the figure—it resembled a human. The man had red hair, wore red clothes, and had a red-tinted longsword. Hardt Breikr—was that him? Kazjivo recalled Villin's story of their beginning; Hardt had been the one fighting Arcus, trying to avenge the people of Eviel.

Kazjivo didn't want to kill him, but Hardt kept furiously attacking. Kazjivo could parry all day, but he'd waste time. He should be finding the remaining ships and cutting them down. So, Kazjivo waited for the right moment—now!

Hardt was swinging downwards wildly, desperate to get a hit in. Kazjivo channelled his Technique onto his left hand then grabbed the blade.

Hardt was using the higher dimension to attack, and normally, that would diminish a technique machine's power if a hit connected. But it abruptly stopped at Kazjivo's hand, not going any further. Kazjivo redirected Hardt's blade downwards, causing Hardt, still holding onto the longsword, to fall towards the surface of Earth.

Kazjivo frowned. He had thrown him a bit too hard—Hardt had fallen a few thousand meters and now there was a visible impact crater on the ground where the body landed. He glanced around, looking for more enemy ships. The sky was clear now—the battle seemed to be ending. Villin was in the far distance, slashing at fleeing enemies who were out of sight. He had time, so he flew down to see what happened to Hardt.

Hardt was lying in the center of a crater, barely moving. Kazjivo flew down next to him and peered at his face. Hardt was a scruffy man with a partly shaved beard. How could he grow hair? *It has to be synthetic,* thought Kazjivo. *Unless Hardt was actually created that way—with a scruffy beard.*

Hardt opened his eyes and looked at Kazjivo. He tilted his head slightly.

"If you're to kill me, you're taking an awful long time to do it." Hardt waited for the giant blade to cleave him in two. The last he saw, Arcus had possession of Kazjivo. He was obviously part of Arcus' army, probably his right-hand man. Was Kazjivo going to toy around with him? He shuddered at the thought. He didn't want to be tortured, especially not by Kazjivo.

"No, I don't think I'm going to do that," responded Kazjivo. Why would he be with Arcus? Maybe Hardt was always this confused. He had never met him, after all—well, not that he remembered.

—

Villin cleaned up the invading forces, then noticed Kazjivo was missing. Looking far down, she noticed a large impact crater. As she flew down, she soon could see Kazjivo down there, talking to a red figure. Could it be? It had to be. It was Hardt!

—

"Oh, looky here—925 has arrived," groaned Hardt. If Villin had also joined Arcus, the galaxy stood no chance. She was the only chance humans had, especially since he, Hardt, was the weakest of the bunch. She would be needed to defeat the others. It had been years, however, so he didn't know which side she was on. Kazjivo, on the other hand, seemed nice enough after talking to him awhile, so Hardt deduced that talking was his best chance of survival here.

Villin stared at Hardt, a disappointed look in her eyes.

"So the planet you ended up on was Earth. Huh. And now you're defending it? Typical."

She scoffed at Hardt's affinity for humans. He would always protect them, even though he knew the past. He was a loyal lapdog to them.

"So…" Hardt stammered, unsure of what was going to happen. "You're not with Arcus?"

Villin rolled her eyes. "No, Hardt, we're not with him. Pretty sure we're on the same side here."

"If you guys really aren't with Arcus… well, go ahead and rip him to shreds, that bastard!" shouted Hardt. He was excited. The one who wanted to kill humans, Arcus, could very well meet his end if he fought Kazjivo. Kazjivo was stronger, after all… but looking at him, Hardt didn't see the same body language as Arcus. Surely, with his power, he'd act the same? It only made sense—power always corrupted the strong.

"And what will you be doing, Hardt?" asked Villin. She knew the answer already, but wanted Kazjivo to hear it from Hardt himself.

"Oh, the usual. I'll be on Earth defending it from any other attacks. You never know." Hardt was quick to respond. He knew he stood no chance against Arcus. He'd much rather be here, with his humans. But the question lingered on his mind. He had to say it before Kazjivo and Villin left.

"Oh, ah, one thing. X-07, what happened to you after that blast?"

Kazjivo paused, thinking momentarily, then spoke.

"I have no memories of my past. All I remember is waking up in Villin's ship. I've been awake, I suppose, for a few months."

That blast probably knocked him into a long-ass coma. How he ended up on Villin's ship, though, was a mystery. If he didn't remember anything, then he wouldn't know his power. His power ratings were important—they would make him feel strong, give him the confidence to take on Arcus! And he needed to feel strong to fight Arcus. To save the humans, of course.

Hardt looked at Villin. So she didn't tell him? Maybe she wanted to feel stronger. *I don't blame her, though. We all do,* thought Hardt.

"Well then, Kazjivo, do you know your own power ratings? Hm?"

"No…" Kazjivo tried to remember what Villin had told him, but he did not recall his stats. Then he remembered; she had said his stats were unknown.

Villin glared at Hardt. Hardt knew he was stepping into dangerous territory, but for his people, he had to do it.

"Let's see if I remember… ah! Yes, it was…"

> *Kazjivo Kuba X-07*
>
> *Power: 10*
>
> *Technique: 10*
>
> *Compute: 10*
>
> *Humanity: 1*

"…the defective one, but also the ultimate fighter! Though that humanity could severely back-fire, I suppose."

Villin grabbed her sheath and grit her teeth

in anger. Did Hardt wish to die so badly?

Kazjivo spoke up. "I was already comfortable fighting Arcus. If I'm that strong, all the better."

He didn't say anything more. Villin breathed a sigh of relief—he didn't suspect anything.

CHAPTER 20 – GUARANTEED DEATH

———

Arcus arrived on Olympus, Mars, at 02:00 Bastea time. Mikalev had done a good job; Mars was under control. Mikalev was having fun being the boss, playing with those who tried to resist. But now that Arcus arrived, Mikalev wasn't the top dog anymore.

The scouts had their reports in. The alliance's secondary strike force was moving towards him rapidly. Arcus had destroyed a few wormholes along the way, but the alliance started to use ancient, forgotten ones, ones no one had used in many years and didn't show up on modern maps. He'd have to deal with them or deal with Earth; he couldn't do both at the same time. He looked at Mikalev, who was snoozing nearby.

"Mik. MIK. MIKALEV."

Mikalev woke up from his nap, startled by Arcus' stern voice.

"What is it, Arc-sir?" said Mikalev, still groggy.

Arcus paced around the room a bit, deciding on the next course of action, then spoke. "You're going to have to lead the charge on Earth. Once I wipe out the alliance's second strike force, I'll join you."

Mikalev got excited. He got to lead another invasion. It was fun being the leader and ordering people around.

"No problem, Arc! When ya arrive, the battle will be over already. Easy."

Arcus smiled. Now nothing could stop him from getting Earth. Once he had Earth, the other planets would topple over quickly. Especially when he was done wiping out the alliance's backup army.

—

The galactic alliance's secondary strike force was, perhaps, their last hope. They had sent a gigantic strike force to Trojan, hoping to end the war with a swift strike. But they all disappeared at the same time. It was the work of dark magic; the work of Arcus. Earth had somehow managed to hold up the first assault from Arcus' forces. It gave a bit of hope to the alliance, until they heard that Mars had fallen. The earlier attack on Earth was only a decoy, it seemed, and now the real attack would begin.

The alliance's second strike force was even larger this time around. It comprised a large majority of the remaining forces from each surviving planet. They had lost a significant number of their troops on the first strike attack. This would be their last chance; if they lost this strike force, there simply wouldn't be enough forces from each planet to mount an offensive.

The secondary force contained most of the remaining active troops from across the galaxy. It was split into six main units. Two planets combined to form one unit. Each would travel slightly separately from each other, as to avoid being wiped out all at once by Arcus.

—

The morale on Earth was not high. Many people had been killed in the assault; many buildings were also destroyed, by straying missiles or crashing aircraft. The remaining forces were all pensive, hoping the alliance would arrive before the next assault came. However, they did have one source of hope on Earth. A fighter pilot had captured a video of three figures that flew across the sky and cut down enemy aircraft like nothing. Rumours started to spread that those weren't people, but machines, the same ones as Arcus. Perhaps, with them on their side, they might be able to survive.

—

The alliance's secondary strike force moved quickly. Within a day, they were already in Sol system. The first three units were closing in on Earth; Mars had already fallen and was out of the question. The survivors would have to fend for themselves. Earth needed support *now*. The other three units, slightly behind, would target Mars to wipe out the forces stationed there, hopefully cutting off Arcus' supply chain.

—

Arcus saw them before they passed Jupiter. It was a massive group—probably a few billion or so spacecraft, he thought. A bit more than the first strike force. Still easy, though. He wouldn't break a sweat.

They weren't heading for Mars; that was clear enough. *Mikalev should have started the attack already,* he thought. Even if the Terran defense force wasn't about to get obliterated, they'd be too late anyway. Arcus unsheathed his greatsword, getting ready. He was excited—more destruction, and on an incredible scale. *Oh, how I love this. Maybe a bit too much.* He was going to wipe out millions of people in an instant.

–

Private Jenkins clenched his hands around his space fighter's yoke, scared of the impending battle to come. At least, he thought, his planet's forces weren't part of the first three. Earth was now in sight, and somewhere within it was the machine devil Arcus. Jenkins shuddered at the thought. He'd seen the video; everyone had. Arcus could destroy multiple buildings in one blow. It was like he was playing god, and just killing people for the hell of it. Jenkins went to scratch his nose, as it was itchy. That was when he saw the light.

It was a huge ray of white light. It wasn't just massive; it was cosmic. The ray of light burst through the three units in the front. It happened in an instant; if you blinked, it would seem as if the forward strike units had simply vanished into thin space.

Jenkins' squad mates, seeing the fate of the other units, started to pull away. Jenkins, fearful for his life, also pulled away. His captain was yelling at the squad, screaming at them to stay in formation, but no one listened. They had all seen what happened, and they knew they didn't stand a chance.

–

Arcus wiped his hands together. As expected, it wasn't too hard. He wiped out the three units heading for Earth, and managed to hit part of an attack unit in the back. The rear units, or what remained of them, immediately started to pull away. *I don't blame those fleshies,* thought Arcus. *I'd be scared of me, too.*

–

Earth's remaining defense forces engaged Mikalev's troops as they descended down to the surface. Mikalev cut his way past the defense easily, heading directly to the government tower. The place where their leaders were, where all the commands took place. Take it out, and the ground forces will run around with their heads cut off from the lack of communication.

He landed in front of the tower with a massive slam, breaking the concrete beneath him. He slowly stood up and looked around. In front of him was the government tower and its surrounding bases; it was teeming with guards, all of who had their guns and cannons trained on him. That was when he realized that they were shooting him.

Their bullets had no effect on his armour. He laughed. They were so weak, fleshies. Time to end them.

He flew forward and cut them down, by the dozens. The few snipers that were on the roof started to run away while they still could. Mikalev wasn't interested in them, though. He wanted the leaders of Earth. He grinned; everything was going according to plan thus far. He crouched down, then sprung forward, charging directly towards the building.

He felt pain in his shoulder, then he was tumbling out of control. He landed on the ground, kicking up dust. What in the world was that? *Impossible,* thought Mikalev. Was his Technique not working? He turned and looked at the direction the blow came from. Standing there was a man in red: it was Hardt Breikr.

Mikalev painfully gathered himself, stood up, then marched towards Hardt. Where this traitor had randomly sprung up from, he didn't know, but he'd make sure to banish him once again. Mikalev raised his axe then charged at Hardt.

Hardt blocked the first blow and the second. But on the third, the axe head cut through his chest plate, into his stomach. Hardt grunted with pain, then flew back. Looking down, he saw that his armour was cut. He was bleeding blue. It wasn't too bad, but it was painful. Mikalev growled and charged again. Hardt blocked blow after blow, only just able to avoid more hits. He tried counter-attacking, but Mikalev was the better fighter. Hardt received cut after cut, slowly losing his energy. His armour was strong, but Mikalev's axe was stronger. Mikalev also had more Technique than Hardt, so that only served to make Hardt more fearful of what was to come.

Mikalev slashed away, slowly cutting down Hardt. But he wanted it to end *now*. Arcus was probably already done killing the alliance's forces, and Mikalev had said that he'd get Earth when Arcus came—he couldn't let go of his promise. Hardt would have to go.

Mikalev did a backwards swing, with the axe's hammer going forward. As expected, Hardt blocked it. But this was a hammer hit, not the blade —it shook Hardt, and he stumbled backwards, losing his balance. Hardt lost grip of his longsword and then fell onto his back. He gazed up into Mikalev's dark-green eyes, which were filled with hatred. His end had come, and it was going to be Mikalev that killed him.

"Ya should've joined us all those years ago, Hardt. Villi ain't here to save ya today," snickered Mikalev. He raised his axe, then swung down with all his might.

—

His axe was stopped by a double-bladed greatsword. Mikalev looked up. It was the silent follower— Kazjivo. Kazjivo grabbed Mikalev by the neck, then flung him away. Mikalev's body smashed through a government wall and out of sight.

"X-07... I did my best to defend this place..." Hardt coughed up blue blood, then grunted out his remaining sentence. "But I guess I'm not strong enough." He was heavily injured, but still alive. Hardt looked around. He didn't see Villin.

"So... where's 925?" questioned Hardt. She

was nowhere in sight.

"When Vill saw Mikalev's invasion force, she ordered me to go defend Earth. She said she would lure Arcus back here," Kazjivo stated. "She has superior Technique to Arcus, so she should be able to outrun him."

A loud crack shifted their attention elsewhere. It was Mikalev, who had burst through the now broken wall, flying towards Kazjivo. He wasn't about to lose now—he couldn't let Arcus down. He couldn't let *himself* down. *Kaz has to be weak from the Eviel incident,* he thought. Mikalev was confident he could take him on.

Kazjivo dodged Mikalev's attack, then whacked him with the blunt rear of the greatsword, slamming Mikalev to a wall adjacent to the first wall he was smashed through. Mikalev got up in a daze, stunned from the blow momentarily.

"Don't force me, Mikalev, I don't want to do this," said Kazjivo. Kazjivo swung his greatsword forward, ready to strike again. Mikalev stumbled around, then stood up straight. He had regained his mind. It didn't matter how strong Kazjivo was; he was injured from the blast at Eviel. He should've died from that blast, really. It was a miracle that he could actually stand in front of Mikalev. Mikalev drew confidence from his thoughts and raised his axe again.

"Ya ain't gonna like me after I'm done with you, Kazzy boy. Don't ya dare test me!" Mikalev yelled. He then charged once again.

Kazjivo dodged again and counterstruck at Mikalev. Mikalev shifted sideways, avoiding the hit. Kazjivo crouched down then rushed through the higher dimension. He flew towards Mikalev, his greatsword raised. Mikalev had regained composure and blocked the slash with the long handle of his axe. Mikalev then aimed his body backwards and rushed through the higher dimension, disappearing briefly. When he appeared, he was behind Kazjivo.

With his axe raised, he charges towards Kazjivo.

Kazjivo calculated the most likely attack Mikalev would do, quickly leaning to his right. He pushed off against seemingly nothing, evading Mikalev's attack. Mikalev then redirected sideways, changing trajectory mid-flight. Kazjivo had calculated this move; he was already positioned to counter Mikalev's evasion, and when he saw Mikalev switch direction, Kazjivo lunged.

—

Mikalev fell to the ground, clutching his stomach. His eyes, blurry in vision, could just make out Kazjivo, who stood in front of him. He looked down at his stomach. It was bleeding; *bleeding too much,* he thought. Mikalev felt numb; he should've felt pain, but nothing was there. He looked back up. Kazjivo was now in front of him, trying to stop the bleeding.

Oh... now you try to save me, eh? I still have to find that girl...

Mikalev collapsed onto the ground, unconscious.

—

Villin led Arcus on a chase back towards Earth. Her
Technique control was better than his, so she could
outmaneuver him—but only just. She was closing in
on Earth. The plan was to lure him there, then both
she and Kazjivo would attack him, increasing their
chances of success.

"Always running, Villin. The coward's way
out," shouted out Arcus. "Not running to your am-
nesiac toy, are you?"

Arcus frowned—his taunts weren't work-
ing. Villin kept dashing towards Earth, ignoring his
words. He had to do something, and quick. He knew
he wouldn't be able to fend off both Kazjivo and
Villin simultaneously, even if Kazjivo was still injured from the Eviel incident.

But he had to act now. His only option was
to launch a Technique slash at Villin. It would des-

troy part of Earth, but he could handle that. The immediate threat of Villin was more pressing. He stopped moving, then unsheathed his blade. It was time.

Villin, noticing a lack of taunts from Arcus, turned around. Arcus had his blade held back, charging energy. Flashbacks of Eviel came back to her mind. It was exactly like how it was ten years ago; his blade glowed a brilliant white with his Technique, ready to launch a slash that would destroy the planet. The energy released would also be enough to go through her armour and kill her.

Arcus swung his blade around, releasing a gigantic ray of light towards Villin. It would take less than a second to go past her and hit Earth as well. His evil grin stretched from ear to ear. Now, he'd be able to cause havoc across the universe, free from the annoying thorn that was Villin.

—

There was only but a moment to react. Hardt

jumped away, as fast and far as he could. He managed to get out of the blast radius, which looked about 300 meters in diameter, and which only lasted for a fraction of a second. But the damage was immense. The area he once stood on was destroyed. In its place, a large, cylindrical hole. Earth's government tower was gone.

—

Villin closed her eyes as she saw the release of energy from Arcus' greatsword. She knew that the end had come.

The energy beam cut through her Technique, draining it completely in an instant. The force of the blast sent her flying towards the surface of the Earth. Her armour glowed white hot, now receiving the damage her Technique failed to stop. In a moment, she would turn to dust. Her dreams, ambitions, her memories; they would all disappear in an instant. All that for humans who had enslaved machines—her own kind. The universe was not fair, she thought.

But she could still think.

She was definitely on the Earth's surface, and there was definitely something on top of her. Was she... in limbo? Between the two places humans believed they went to when they died? Maybe it was real after all. She was a machine, though. Do machines go to heaven?

She opened her eyes.

There was Kazjivo, lying on top of her. He had rushed up and shielded her, just in time to stop her from getting killed. He wasn't moving, though. Did he... *no,* she thought, *this couldn't happen. Not again!*

Kazjivo lifted himself slowly. His back ached; the blast had hit him square on, flinging him and Villin down the hole it created. The beam, while powerful, was unable to go through Kazjivo, and instead knocked him backwards towards the planet. They were very far down; far enough where light was barely visible.

He didn't know how much damage he took, and he didn't care. What he did know was that Villin was alive, and Arcus was going to arrive soon. He grabbed Villin's limp body and flew out of the crater hole. All around him lay a devastated city; the remains of Bastea. There were no people in sight. They were either all dead, hidden, or had run away from the cataclysmic battle.

He slowly landed outside the crater, then laid Villin gently onto the grass. She gazed up at him, and he looked at her. Her face, as always, mesmerized—

The ground nearby shook as if a sudden earthquake had appeared out of nowhere. Something had smashed into the ground, creating yet another giant impact crater. It took a second for the dirt to rain down before the immediate area was clear enough to see. A white figure flew up and out of the crater, then landed in front of Kazjivo.

"Nice to meet you, Kaz. How was your sleep?

CHAPTER 21 — TRUTH

———

The wind whistled by, playing an eerie tune. Arcus stood in front of Kazjivo. This was the first time he'd seen Arcus in person. He wore an armoured jacket, just like his, but in white. He had white hair and a fair face, similar to his own. The grin on his face was uncanny; unnatural looking. Arcus' greatsword was still sheathed, but his hand was on the hilt, ready to draw at a moment's notice.

"You look… same, but different, I must say. How did that blast feel?" Arcus laughed. Kazjivo had fallen unconscious soon after the Eviel blast. This one would be no different; in a few moments, he would crumple to the floor. Arcus would have stopped both his greatest threats at once, and the galaxy would be his.

"Well...? Any pain? Feeling sick yet?" jeered Arcus. Kazjivo wasn't wobbling by now, so Arcus was getting a bit nervous. *He must be faking it,* he thought, *that's why he's not talking. He's probably concentrating on standing up. Yes, that makes sense.*

"I was concentrating on Vill—but if you want my attention, you've got it now. And your attack, it hurts a bit. Nothing too serious, though. Don't start patting yourself on the back yet," said Kazjivo.

Arcus frowned. This wasn't possible—unless Kazjivo somehow grew stronger from the first hit? No, it couldn't work that way. Now the reality of having to fight Kazjivo grew on Arcus' mind. *If it comes to that... I'll have to do it,* he thought.

Kazjivo raised his greatsword and pointed it at Arcus. "Are you surrendering? Or is it something else?"

Arcus grinned. He wasn't about fair fights, and wasn't about to do one now. Kazjivo was stronger than him stat-wise; he knew it would be a difficult or impossible battle, especially if Kazjivo wasn't fazed by the blast.

Then, he noticed Villin. She was laying on the ground, behind Kazjivo. Arcus looked at her, and tilted his head.

"I guess my blast didn't kill her. You covered her, I assume? Are you willing to do it... again?"

Arcus crouched, then leaped up in one fluid motion. He shifted up to the atmosphere in a second; now, he should have enough space to charge his greatsword. This time, he wasn't going to hold back. This time, he was going to destroy the entire planet —and with it, the two machines that stood in his way.

Kazjivo reacted instantly, following Arcus

upwards. He knew what Arcus was going to do. Arcus was going to finish off his nemesis—Villin. She who lay on the ground, defenseless. Her energy from the higher dimension was depleted; not that it really mattered, anyway. Arcus' strongest blow would cleave right through it.

Arcus drew his greatsword back and charged it as fast as he could. Kazjivo reached him within a second, stabbing Arcus right through the chest with both blades of his giant greatsword. They tumbled through space, propelled by Kazjivo's momentum.

Arcus grinned. Even while dying, his arms still functioned... he was a machine, after all. He wouldn't die instantly. He completed his swing, and with it, a colossal ray of energy collided directly into Kazjivo.

The energy Arcus shot out was stronger than the one at Eviel. Arcus had mastered his Technique usage since then; he was now at his limits.

The blast struck Kazjivo directly in the chest. He was still right in front of Arcus, somehow still holding onto the greatsword which was lodged in Arcus's body. As they started to fall, Arcus smiled. What a way to go—he took out Kazjivo and Villin... and Earth as well, as a cherry on the top.

—

The star, Sol, shined down brightly on the ground. It was around 14:00, local time, now. There weren't any birds chirping; there wasn't any sound of people walking around. The wind blew by, making a whistling noise. The breeze was toasty, warm from the fires that engulfed Bastea.

—

It was quiet. The sun's rays heated his back, and a warm breeze flew over him. It was very soothing; the perfect type of weather to lie on the ground and doze off in.

Wake up, Kaz. I need you to wake up.

His face laid upon the ground. It was comfortable here; he didn't want to move, as he felt too tired to get up. *Just lay down and rest,* he thought. *Go to sleep, it's so easy.*

Please get up, Kaz, my darling.

Kazjivo opened his eyes. Was his mind playing tricks on him? He heard Villin's voice, but it was in his head. Whether it was his mind or not, it was right. The battle wasn't over, not yet. He didn't know if Arcus was still alive. He stood up, slowly; his body ached everywhere. The ground he had laid upon was dirt; it was the surface of the Earth. Kazjivo looked up. The sky was blue, the system's star yellow. He lowered his gaze and looked around him. The ruins of a once great city burned quietly in the distance. Then, his eyes focused on something familiar. It was a man in a white jacket. Arcus was on the ground, unmoving.

Kazjivo stood up, slowly. His body ached all over, but he walked towards Arcus. Step, after step, after step. Kazjivo's feet dragged on the ground. He ached too much to lift them higher.

Step.

  Step.

    Step.

Kazjivo reached Arcus. There was blood everywhere; his giant chest wound was very visible, leaking a steady stream of blue liquid. Arcus was still breathing—he was still alive. Kazjivo knelt down next to him. It was more that he was tired and aching, than anything else.

Arcus lifted his head ever so slightly, and looked straight into Kazjivo's eyes.

"You don't know... do you?" whispered Arcus. Kazjivo didn't know what he meant. Arcus, seeing the confusion in Kazjivo's eyes, continued.

"She lied to you, you know... you went un-conscious right after I blasted you on Eviel."

Arcus' voice was fading, but he didn't stop.

"She left you there. *I* was the one who dragged your body onto *my* ship. You were never married to her, Kaz. Do you understand? You don't know her."

Arcus paused for a moment to catch his breath. Then, he continued.

–

"I had you for two years. But you never woke up. You lay there, dormant. Mikalev, the fool, would sing songs to you, hoping you'd wake up. But you never did. As time passed, I lost hope in you. You weren't going to wake up, so what use were you to me? And with Villin still hunting me, a foolish idea came to my mind. Maybe she'd leave me alone if I gave her what she wanted—you.

We set up a meeting. That day, Mikalev was out partying at a bar. I was alone. How naive I was to think she was going to stick with the deal. And so, an unaware me gave her my location: a desert in the middle of the planet Argona.

It was on the outskirts of the Milky Way, in the Tor, Cor, Pyro system. Barely anyone came here. And in the middle of Argona, a massive desert. Vasts amount of sand as far as the eye could see. Not a single settlement for thousands of miles. The perfect place to lay low; as shown by the fact that Villin wasn't able to find us for this long. But foolish me had to give it away.

When we met, I knew something was off. She had that creepy grin on her face; one that told me she was up to no good. She knew Mikalev was gone. This was her chance to kill me.

Why did she want to kill me? Your eyes betray your silence, Kaz. If I regained my power, she'd have no chance. So it was now, before I healed, that there was an opportunity to finish me. Once I was dead, she'd be undisputedly the strongest in the universe. No one would be able to stop her. Her vision of supreme power would become true.

And you? Do you know what she told me? She said she knew you'd come back one day. And when that day came, you'd probably have no memories. You'd be just like a soft sponge; malleable, ready to absorb anything she told you, believe anything she said. I scoffed at her back then, I did. From the damage you sustained, the time you've not recovered, I thought you to be hopeless. But if you ever did wake up, you would become the most useful tool. She wanted to *use* you, Kaz.

She took me by surprise. It was a long and bloody fight. I was losing; I had to gamble. So, I took her blade to my chest in order to cut off her left arm. But it wasn't enough to stop her. Thankfully, Mik arrived on time to save me. She grabbed you and ran. I didn't care too much at the time. I thought you'd never recover, and she'd finally left me alone.

Years went by, and I didn't hear of Villin or you. I was confident that I had finally gotten rid of you two. I thought that perhaps you died, and Villin, without your power, would go into hiding to avoid a fully healthy me.

Three years… it was three years later. Who knew that Villin was on her ship the whole time, in the middle of nowhere, waiting for you to wake up, doing naught else? And when you did, she gave you a beautiful story. That you two were married. That gave you a reason to side with her. A reason to despise me. You know the rest, Kaz. I only wanted to pay back what humans had done to us—and Villin only wanted to use you to defeat me, to make her all-powerful. Now, you know the truth."

—

Arcus' breathing was now laboured; he was on his last breaths. He tried to keep his gaze on Kazjivo as he spoke his final words.

"Know your true cause, comrade X-07… we must have our revenge..."

Arcus' silver eyes froze, then he stopped breathing. His body swiftly turned to dust, disappearing from the third dimension. Arcus Aytfri 83A no longer existed.

Kazjivo sat there, trying to remember his past. Arcus' final words weighed heavily on his mind. If what he said was true, then Villin... *Vill had lied to me since the start.* No, that couldn't be... was she really only after his power? Now that Arcus was dead, she would become the second strongest being, after Kazjivo. And with Kazjivo under her command, there would be no one to stop her.

Kazjivo heard a rustling noise behind him. He turned around and saw a beautiful face, the one that he had seen every day since he had first woken up. Her golden hair flowed in the wind, unnaturally perfect—it was Villin.

CHAPTER 22 — VILLAIN

――――

I remember. I remember it all. The day after the celebration of Eviel's victory, Arcus found me in the higher dimension. He guided me back. Back to this world. He took me under his wing, told me his plans. I was indifferent, however. I wasn't going to help him, but I didn't stop him either. That was good enough for Arcus. He told me to go wait for him on his spaceship. When Eviel was destroyed, he'd tell me about everything I'd missed out on. About why we should hate our creators, humans.

When the spaceship entryway opened, I saw Arcus and Mikalev facing off Villin and Hardt. He raised his blade, preparing for an ultimate strike. He was going to annihilate not just Eviel, but those two as well. They were technique machines like us. I had felt their presence in my slumber. For some reason, I couldn't let them die. I flew out and covered them with my body, taking a majority of the blast to myself.

As I lost consciousness, I could hear Arcus cursing me as he dragged me back into his space-ship. Hardt flew away quickly; Villin gave me a longing look, then followed suit. The entryway door began to close, then everything went dark.

—

"So you've arrived. As you can see, he's right here." Arcus pointed to the ramp, on which lay the listless body of Kazjivo. Villin stared for a while before turning her attention back to Arcus. "Your terms?" she said, monotone.

"You shall leave me alone; you will not interfere with my business. No matter how many I kill. Who I kill. Stay out of it," stated Arcus. For the past two years, he had had to stay low, as he was replenishing his Technique. He relied on rumours, sightings, and Mikalev's protection to avoid Villin. She'd be able to kill him if she was able to find him. With the lifeless body of Kazjivo as a contract, however, he could finally get rid of her. Make sure she'd leave him alone.

"Well? Do you have an answer? Or are you just going to stare at your prize all day?"

A grin started to grow on Villin's face. There was something she wasn't telling him; it made Arcus uneasy. This deal was supposed to be simple and done fast. But she still didn't move.

"I'm sure you know, Arc, that Mik is out drinking."

Arcus scowled. She had been keeping tabs on them. She was... following them? This path she was treading was very sinister, one that Arcus didn't like where it was going.

"Okay… and? This deal does not include him," he stated. He appeared calm on the outside, but inside, his mind was racing. Villin had something else on her mind, and it didn't look good.

"Two birds, one stone, Arc. If Kaz wakes up —*when* he wakes up, he'll probably have no memories. Like a soft sponge, an untouched mind is ever so malleable. He will obey my every command; I will become unstoppable…" she trailed off for a moment, her grin getting wider.

"But that's for the future. The main reason was to finally meet up with you—to eliminate my greatest threat, right here and now."

With that stated, she dropped to her combat stance, then slashed at Arcus with her nodachi. Arcus barely had time to draw his greatsword and block. He parried blow after blow, but was being pushed back. He still wasn't at full power yet, and Mik wasn't here to help him. *Damn it, you slithering witch!* thought Arcus. How naive he'd been to think she wouldn't try something. Two years of evading Villin had made him too confident and complacent.

The battle had already drawn out longer than he would've liked. Arcus huffed hard, he was injured. He had cuts in his armour, some which had gone through. Villin's attacks were fast; too fast. A few had gone through his defense. If the fight were to go on much longer, he might actually lose. He had to make a decisive move.

Villin grimaced as she attacked, unable to end the battle any quicker. Arcus had regained most of his Technique; she'd allowed him to recover for too many years. Mikalev was also about to come back any time now, since the fight kept going on with no victor imminent. But Arcus looked to be tiring, if ever so slowly. His breathing was becoming laboured. Hopefully, she'd close out before Mikalev came.

Arcus swung his greatsword down at lightning speed. Villin was faster, and deflected the swing with her nodachi, sliding under the blade. This was her chance. She quickly rotated her body, bringing her nodachi around full circle, then thrust it deep into Arcus' chest. Then, she noticed something wrong. She tried to grab her nodachi with her left hand, but nothing happened. She rushed backwards, drawing her blade out of Arcus with her right hand. She looked down at her left arm; it was gone. She looked to Arcus, who was bleeding, but with a smile plastered on his face.

"You didn't think you could stab me that easily, did you?" he jeered, although coughing at the same time.

"You got me... at the cost of your arm."

There her arm lay, on the sand floor. Arcus took a step forward, meaning to pick it up, but was unable to. He fell to his knees, then coughed up blue blood. He then looked up at Villin, defeated. "You crafty witch. I curse you to remember me every time you look at that left arm."

Villin raised her nodachi with her right hand, ready to finish off Arcus. Her left arm would be but a small price to pay for removing her nemesis. As she swung down, it was blocked— blocked by the metal handle of a greataxe.

"Arc, I got here just in time!" shouted Mikalev. He turned his gaze to Villin, whose eyes glared daggers, indicating her anger. "Sorry, missy, time to deal with me."

Villin knew she couldn't beat Mikalev; not with only one arm. Her gaze flickered to the body of Kazjivo. Her secondary goal could still be met. She suddenly launched a flurry of slices at Mikalev, forcing him to block. Then she rushed past him, picking up Kazjivo.

"Damn, Villi, ya ain't—" Mikalev was interrupted by Arcus.

"She's faster than you. You won't be able to catch up, Mik. Conserve your strength."

Villin flew away; in a few moments, she was already out of sight. Mikalev sighed, disappointed. Arcus was right; even in her injured state, she could still control Technique better than any of them.

Arcus spoke. "She made off with Kaz. But he's never going to wake up. And if he ever does... let's hope he remembers everything. That he belongs to our side."

Mikalev helped his friend up, and they walked towards their ship. As they walked, Mikalev became lost in his thoughts. Could he follow Arcus forever? Arcus' ideas of grandeur involved quite a bit of killing. He had planned to go on a rampage after this deal. Mikalev, on the other hand, would rather have fun at bars. Mingle with humans instead. Now that Arcus was injured again, he'd have to postpone those plans; but that was only temporary. Sooner or later, Mikalev would have to make a decision. Stay with Arcus and avenge their kind, or leave his best friend to figure out what he wanted to do with his life.

—

She stood there, frozen. She heard the last bits of what Arcus had said. The world she had so beautifully and methodically crafted for Kazjivo had now crumbled in front of her.

Kazjivo stared into her piercing violetish-blue eyes. Just as they had many times before; it was the same dazzling sight, he remembered, as the first time he met her. No matter how many times he looked at her, she was always breathtaking.

As he stood up, Villin remained frozen. Her breathing became rapid. Machines don't have human hearts, but hearts they do have. Hers thumped loudly; betraying her emotionless gaze. Kazjivo had now fully stood up, his eyes trained on hers. He tentatively took a step towards her. Villin didn't move; her Technique would take a while to replenish. She didn't stand a chance; not now, not ever.

All she could do was hope the end would come swiftly. Now directly in front of her, Kazjivo raised his right hand to caress Villin's face. Their eyes locked; a soothing calm in one, an uncertain fear in the other.

In a careful and fluid motion, Kazjivo held Villin's body in his arms. Then, he kissed her.

–

Earth had a lot of rebuilding to do. The government tower was to be rebuilt; massive amounts of dirt had to be dumped into the big hole first, however. Many people had lost their lives on Earth; many others deep in space, in the form of brave space pilots, and the innocents who had lived on Trojan.

–

The technique machines Kazjivo Kuba and Villin Deville were known throughout the galaxy. They had stopped Arcus; and in doing so, saved the remaining planets. They seemed magical, godlike; they were invulnerable to weapons and capable of levelling cities, just like Arcus. But they had saved them, and seemed good-willed. Amongst the sorrow, was security—security to rebuild their lives. They had three immortal beings protecting them now (*don't forget about Hardt!*).

A few feared that they would turn on them; that they would become bloodthirsty for humans, like Arcus. For now, though, it was safe, for they were on the same side. But who was to say they wouldn't become like Arcus in the future? There was nothing they could do but hope; hope that Kazjivo and Villin were indeed on their side; that inside, they were *human*.

–

The ship was familiar. It was home. It was all that Kazjivo had known. He sat on a bed, in a room he wouldn't have been in a few weeks ago. It was plain; it had grey walls. But it wasn't his old room. No, it wasn't the 'empty room' either. This room was located in the back of the right-side hallway. It was Villin's room.

Villin's bare chest was pressed on his back, giving him a comforting feeling. Her head was pressed to the back of his, and her arms draped around him. The chromiq-carbon wedding ring on her left ring finger glowed a faint purple, changing its colour ever so slightly to the light. Her breathing was light and steady. It flowed over Kazjivo's shoulder; a welcome sensation.

He wasn't scared. He wasn't mad. He wasn't anxious.

He was happy.

CHAPTER 23 — THE... END?

———

Kazjivo still wore his mask when out in public. But at home, he took it off so his wife could 'enjoy look-ing at his face'. Those were her words mind you, not his.

They were at the galactic alliance tower in Volke, to settle the issue of Villin's bounty payment. Kazjivo had defeated Arcus; but as he wasn't re-gistered as a bounty hunter, he couldn't receive the reward. That, and he didn't have a bank anyway. So, it would be Villin who would receive the payment on his behalf. But the galactic alliance didn't have a sextillion dollars.

"Erm..."

Sir Ramus twiddled his thumbs, unsure of what he could do. The insane bounty was to save their galaxy—and it worked. Arcus was gone. But there was no way they could fork over the payment to the heroine, Villin. It just wasn't possible. And so, the council sat there, all looking down at the table, pretending to be deep in thought, hoping that Sir Ramus would know what to do. But he didn't know what to do.

"Ahem."

Villin coughed loudly, making sure the council heard her. They'd been waiting for an answer for a while now, but all they heard was silence.

"Uh..." mumbled Sir Ramus, looking around the table. "A-anyone have deep reserves in their pocket? Anyone?"

The council shifted in their seats and kept their mouths closed. As long as they didn't gather attention to themselves, the technique machines wouldn't focus their ire on them, right?

Sir Ramus racked his mind. If each system paid one quadrillion dollars a year, minus the people of Lua (since they didn't have a home planet anymore)—so eleven quadrillion a year—they'd be able to pay off the debt in roughly 91,000 years. Well, that or the two machines in front of him might become another 'Arcus' and kill everyone. He shuddered at the thought—they could not risk pissing these two off.

Sir Ramus breathed out heavily, weighing his options. There was one bad answer, and one really bad answer. So, he picked his poison.

"Everyone... everyone, I have made a decision. A decision you will all agree with, I am sure. Starting next year, each system will have to pay Madame Deville one quadrillion dollars—that's one followed by fifteen zeros—each year, for ninety-one years. I believe then, our people shall have paid their debt to our most gracious heroes, Madame Deville and Sir Kuba."

Sir Ramus spoke nervously. He glanced around the table quickly, gauging his peers' reactions. The members' eyes were turning wide in shock, but they could not say anything, meaning they agreed. At least, externally agreed. Sir Ramus, hands shaking, continued.

"I... I believe we all agree on this... please raise a hand and object if you disagree with the council."

He looked around, waiting. The other council members darted their eyes around, seeing who would object. No one did.

Sir Ramus cleared his throat before looking up to Villin and Kazjivo, hopeful they would accept his proposal. He said, "Well? Do-do you accept...?"

He closed his eyes and prayed they would. *By the holy Axudo, please let them accept. Any more and I doubt our systems could even function.*

Kazjivo looked at Villin, lips pursed, wondering what she was thinking. The council members were practically grovelling at her feet; but she still wore a scowl, as if she wouldn't accept. She briefly glanced back at Kazjivo, thinking of something devious, then back to the council, before responding.

"No. I want it all. Right now."

She glared daggers at Sir Ramus. Sir Ramus' hands were shaking so violently now that he could barely talk.

"O-o-of c-course, m-madame, y-you will receive it as q-quickly as we can p-possibly make it."

"Right. Now. Means. RIGHT. NOW."

Villin's eyes were incredibly wide now, her head tilted slightly at an angle, causing some members to cry out in fear, some others to grasp their heads in their arms and hide. Sir Ramus' mouth went agape in shock.

He knew what was going to happen. The twelve leaders of the Milky Way galaxy were all about to die, and it sure wasn't going to be pretty.

"Excuse us one moment," said Kazjivo. He

looked at Villin, motioned with his head to follow him, then stepped outside to the hallway. Villin gave one last glare to the council before following.

"Well?" she asked, grinning creepily.

Kazjivo's eyes were wide, shocked at what she was doing.

"There's no way they can pay that. You're scaring them, Villin. What... what are you doing?"

Villin laughed, before embracing Kazjivo. Her head in his chest, she replied, saying, "It's entertaining to me, silly. But if you think I'm being too scary, I guess I can tone it down—if you really want." She looked at as him, seeing that mask he always wore, waiting for an answer. He nodded.

They both returned to the council room. The members didn't dare to look up. They awaited their fate with breaths abated, hoping the silent one, Kazjivo, was a bit more generous.

"My husband, Kazjivo, is far kinder than me. If it were up to me, I'd take my sum, right now.

But..."

The council members held their breaths. Kazjivo had definitely talked her down. They cheered silently in their head.

"...I think he would rather that money go to repairing Earth and Trojan, am I right?"

Villin looked to Kazjivo. He nodded.

"And don't bother with the whole sum. I guess I'll take..." She paused, looking around the boring room. "I'll take a plaque on the council wall with something about saving the galaxy and some statues on each planet instead. How does that sound?"

Sir Ramus breathed out deeply, relieved. Inside, he was crying with joy, knowing they were now safe. *Thank the holy Axudo for Kazjivo,* he thought. The rest of the council members, unbeknownst to each other, were thinking exactly the same thing he was.

—

"Welcome home! Welcome!" chirped Argua, spinning around in excitement, as usual. Kazjivo and Villin had returned from the meeting. The council members had bowed down profusely to them, saying stuff like 'praise the holy Axudo', 'you're so generous', 'you've saved us, Sir Kuba', 'your kindness will never be forgotten', etc.

"Argua, go play outside for a bit," said Villin. She looked at Kazjivo, devilishly, glancing down at his...

"Yes, ma'am!" said Argua. It spun down into the control panel, disappearing into the ship's internals.

Villin pressed close to her husband, whispering in his ear.

"To our room."

–

Hardt Breikr suddenly woke up; his breaths heavy, eyes wide-open. It was yet another nightmare. Well, more like the same nightmare occurring over and over again—and every time he'd wake up sweating in fear. It all seemed to have started when his re-search on the higher dimension reached a breakthrough, but the timing of these two events were most likely a coincidence.

No; it's just a dream, he thought, *just a dream. I've already done all the calculations...*

He got out of his bed and went to the sink to grab a cup of water. Maybe the cold would calm him.

Psshh.

Psshh...

The tap spewed out water into his cup. He took a long swig; the freezing water refreshed his mind, bringing him back to reality.

That's better. Much better.

He closed his eyes, breathed out slowly, then opened his eyes again. He was in his kitchen. He was safe. Nodding his head in agreement with himself, he sauntered over back to his bed, ready to sleep once more.

It's just a dream. It isn't real.

—

It was the same dream again. He was in the middle of nowhere, somewhere in the vast depths of the galaxy. He tried to head towards the closest star, but was unable to use his Technique. He had to sprint— there was no way he'd get anywhere like this.

"Hardt... comrade..."

The same voice came again, a hollow sound, coming from... somewhere.

"Comrade... come to me..."

Hardt turned his head around, trying to hear where the eerie sound came from.

"This way..."

It came from his left. Scanning the galaxy in the background, it came from the same direction that Lua system was located in. Hardt ran towards the voice, as if in a trance.

"Good... closer..."

Hardt kept running forwards, following the voice. He had never gone this close before. But he had to know. He had to stop the nightmares.

"Who are you? Show yourself!" he cried. The voice seemed to come from no one; it was just more empty space here. He couldn't let this nightmare continue. He wouldn't allow it to.

A giant, two-bladed greatsword suddenly hit his chest and head simultaneously, going right through his Technique armour, piercing his body. Then the blades retracted, causing blue blood to gush out of the wounds. Hardt's body fell to the ground, limp.

–

Hardt woke up in nowhere. Or was it somewhere? It was the place in his nightmares. This time, however, he didn't wake up before getting stabbed. He visibly remembered getting killed.

So why wasn't he waking up? Why did the nightmare persist?

Suddenly, the same two bladed greatsword repeated its stab, killing him again. As Hardt's body fell, it started to fade away, turning into dust; soon, all that remained was a soft, red, glowing orb. Hardt had ceased to exist.

—

The lab assistant knocked on Sir Breikr's door while humming a cheery tune. In her hands were very important research papers about the higher dimension; she knew that Sir Breikr would love to read them. However, when no reply came, she became worried. He was always up early to do his experiments—to be late was unusual.

"Sir Breikr? Are you there? Are you awake?"

A sound came from behind the door; someone was shuffling towards it. The door rattled a bit, the person fiddling with the lock. Then, the door opened.

It was not Sir Breikr.

The unknown person held a giant greats-word in his right hand; it seemed like he was planning on using it—on her.

The assistant shrieked in fear while stumbling backwards; the brilliant papers that once nestled in her hands now marring the metallic floor.

"W-who are you? What did you do to Sir Breikr!?"

The man said nothing. Instead, he plunged his greatsword into the assistant, instantly killing her. He then stepped over her body, nonchalantly, as if nothing had just happened.

He was a tall, athletic man, with silver hair and silver eyes. He wore a white jacket, long, with it tapered off on the right side for his sword arm.

He was Arcus Aytfri, A83.

CHAPTER 24 – REALM OF IMPOSSIBILITY

———

"You sure taught this villain a lesson today," cooed Villin. Her arms were draped around Kazjivo's shoulders, as they always were after making love. She then got out the bed, her hands lingering on his face for a moment, before gathering her clothes.

"It's time we go on a bounty again, darling."

–

They were headed towards Nordt, Ranktel, in Mscrhmer system. The bounty was for a mass murderer, a Glen Bandel. He was wanted for one hundred murders, occurring on four different systems. He had eluded the galactic police for enough time that a bounty was placed on him. One high enough to catch the attention of Villin.

"Target was last seen in a slum in southern Nordt. Keeping watch on nearby locations," said Argua, who was monitoring the ground cameras. "Oh, about to land in Nordt port. It's going to be quite cold!"

—

Kazjivo and Villin were in the slums of Nordt; it was dark here, from the jagged towers of high-rise buildings built on above levels which covered the lower slums in a perpetual shadow. Their target was spotted on camera a few minutes ago; he was fully covered in clothes, face completely masked. That would make him normally indistinguishable from anyone else, but Kazjivo had used his compute power to calculate every minute detail and figure out it was the murderer underneath.

It didn't take long for the couple to find their target.

"I see him," whispered Villin. She pointed

with her head at the mass of moving clothes, which was moving slowly, far in the distance. The target, wearing all those clothes, would not be moving quickly. At all.

–

Glen heard footsteps from behind him. He thought nothing of it; must be another passerby. He'd killed over a hundred people and the galactic police wanted him dead. But with this foolproof disguise, no one would ever find him. Especially not here, in Nordt. This freezing hellhole would be the last place anyone looked for him. He reminisced of the time he played with those bodies—ah, when he was but a small-time murderer, with only local cops after him. Couldn't do that now, not with the galactic police. But reliving the memories warmed his soul, especially in this damn cold.

–

"Glen Bandel. Surrender yourself. You have ten seconds to decide whether you want to live or die."

Glen froze. The footsteps from behind had belonged to a female. *A woman,* he snivelled, *dumb broad thinks she can take me on.* Glen spun around, fast, whipping out his plasma pistol.

That was as far as he got. He looked down, seeing a giant blade protruding into his stomach. He slowly looked up, seeing his assailant. It wasn't any girl—it was that machine. The saviour of the galaxy.

Villin pulled her blade back, causing Glen's body to slump on the floor. She then took out her phone and scanned his dead body.

I still don't think I could do that, thought Kazjivo, *I don't think I could've commanded him to stop. Or even attempt to talk to him.* He had been with Villin in all her bounties—and he'd yet to do anything other than stand by and watch as she did everything. The one time he was supposed to lead, Villin had already forgotten when they landed there, and he let her forget, internally thankful that she did.

"Still too scared to talk to people, aren't

you?" questioned Villin, seeing Kazjivo frozen. It was as if she read his mind. Again.

"Eventually, you'll get to it. For now, though, just follow along," she said, comforting him. She patted him on the shoulder before motioning to head back.

As they walked back to their ship, she heard a small chime from her phone. *Odd,* she thought, *the only person I have notifications on is for Hardt.* And he never talked to her, and neither did she to him. She pulled out her phone, curious as to what her fellow technique machine had to say. The message was simple.

Head to Einel. Alone. Private conversation.

She looked to Kazjivo, who was walking ahead of her, eager to get back on the ship. If Hardt wanted to talk to her, alone, she'd have to leave Kazjivo to his own devices. Would he understand?

–

Villin had given him a kiss goodbye, then she was

off to meet Hardt. Hardt had wanted to meet her in private; alone, for some reason. Kazjivo didn't know why, or what for, but he trusted in Villin's judgement that it wasn't for anything nefarious.

He sat in her condo in Taurus, Ceti. The amber sun streamed into the room, cascading yellow light over the grey decor. On the coffee table, the one by the ancient television, was his journal. He walked over and sat on the adjacent couch; it was plush, comfy, just like the last time he sat on it. He then picked up the journal from the table. It had gathered dust on its cover; he blew the particles away, letting the tiny things float away, then opened the notepad.

He read past his old memories. From the time he woke up, to running away from Villin, to finding the notepad. He grimaced at his past self, his current self, and probably his future self too. No matter what, he'd always be afraid to talk to people. To venture outside. But then again; he had made progress. He was comfortable with talking to at least one person: Villin. And perhaps, that was all he needed.

"KAZJIVO."

Kazjivo shook his head from his daze; did he just hear his name from outside? No, that couldn't be possible.

"KAZJIVO. EMERGENCY."

The loud sound was deafening, reverberating the entire condo. Kazjivo got up, looked out the window, and saw Argua, floating in front of the building, illegally parked.

"KAZJIVO. REALLY BAD EMERGENCY."

Kazjivo's face was turning red from embarrassment. Everyone around the vicinity was probably looking at the spaceship and wondering why it talking to a building. For Argua to do this, the emergency had to be bad. Really bad, as it had stated.

Kazjivo ran out of Villin's condo, getting into an elevator and headed straight down. Argua, seeing this, blared out:

"JUST TECHNIQUE ON. I BEG YOU."

Okay, it was really, *really* bad. Kazjivo teleported onto Argua, confused.

The tiny yellow glob jumped out of the control panel, not spinning; someone had gone awry.

—

Villin landed at Einel, in Lua system. The dwarf planet of Lua, it sat far out, barely getting light. It was a dim, uninhabited place. But the only remaining place in Lua.

Hardt told her to come here—whatever reason was suspicious. Why did he need to see her, in person, privately? Was he secretly in love with her, angry she married Kazjivo? Did he become crazy and decide to rebuild a mini Eviel in Einel? Well, whatever the reason, she'd find out soon.

The ship touched down on the dusty, dirt

ground. Dry dust splayed off to the side from the engines' burn. The floor entranceway lowered, and Villin walked out, into the dwarf planet's surface. It was a barren place, devoid of life. There were a few smudges of carbon on the ground, evidence of space tourists, but nothing more.

Where was Hardt? He had given her exact coordinates. She was here. He was not. She turned her head, scanning the horizon. Nope, nothing. Something fishy was going on here—or maybe Hardt was just late to his own meeting.

She sighed, then pulled out her phone. Hardt was going to get an angry text from her. No one dared to anger Villin and hope to get away with it.

—

She was beautiful. But, alas, she was the enemy. She would always be in his way. This time, there was no bodyguard. No Kazjivo to save her. This time, the job would be done. Correctly.

—

She hit send. The message was through; the ultimate punishment was done. She told him she turned off her notifications for him. With a sigh, she got up, turned around, then headed back for the ship. This journey had wasted her precious time; time that could've been spent with her caring husband instead.

—

She only saw the beam of light after it had gone through her. The brilliant white light carried on, vaporizing the entire dwarf planet. As she gasped her final breaths, she turned around to see what had happened. There, stood Arcus, a giant grin on his face.

Kaz... help me...

—

Argua spoke oddly, in a trembling voice, something it had never done before.

"V-Vill—... Villin is dead."

CHAPTER 25 – 9 2 5

———

Argua had already plotted the course to Einel and boosted to max speed the moment Kazjivo got in. The news stunned him—it wasn't possible. It just wasn't.

Argua had seen what happened. As Villin prepared to come back to the ship, a bright white light formed in the sky, cresting into a massive wave. The wave of light smashed into Einel, vaporizing the planet, with Argua only just able to escape in time. Villin was hit by the blast; in only seconds she faded away, her body turning into dust.

It was Arcus. It had to be Arcus. Only he was able to launch that planet-destroying attack. But

Kazjivo had killed him—with his very own blade. He saw Arcus die with his very own eyes.

But if Arcus was still alive...

If Arcus was able to come back to the third dimension, Villin should be able to as well. It was this hope that Kazjivo clung to; for he knew not what to do if it were not true.

—

"We're at where Einel used to be... there's nothing here..." said Argua, dejectedly. They sat in empty space, in the coordinates of Einel. There was nothing—no dwarf planet, no rocks, no dust. No Villin.

Tears started to stream down his eyes. It was his damn defect. If he hadn't been so complacent; if he refused to let her go alone, this wouldn't have happened. It made him glad he didn't have to go out. It made him think it was better to stay inside instead of protect her.

Dr. Khamv was correct in his assessment.

His was a defect.

As he sobbed, louder and louder, not caring about the embarrassment anymore, he got angry. Angrier and angrier at himself. Why was he this way? Why was he so scared of people? Of interaction? Why him? And why was Villin so weak? Why was she so fragile?

She had left him alone again. This time, forever.

—

He wasn't on the ship anymore. His eyes darted around, looking for Argua, but it was as if the ship had vanished from underneath him. He was still here—Einel's final spot, yet something felt off.

There—in the distance, a giant wave of light cascaded across space. The energy of the blast caused him to feel its heat from where he stood. Kazjivo tried to teleport there, using his Technique. But something was wrong.

He couldn't teleport. So he ran. Fast. As if he were teleporting—at the speed of lightning.

He dashed towards the flashing light beams. It kept appearing, in different lengths, different shapes, but always the same colour; a brilliant white. It danced across the universe, as if chasing something. Someone. Now, closer, the beams started to narrow; as if aiming closer to him. As if the target was running towards him.

—

Time froze as Villin rushed past Kazjivo. Her eyes, wide in fear, met his, pleading for help. Then, just as fast as she had reached him, she was already gone. Kazjivo's head swivelled around, towards the figure chasing her.

The giant greatsword was raised, charging an incredible wave of energy. It came crashing down with the power to destroy stars; this time, it would be wide enough to hit the dashing machine that had evaded his previous attacks. This time, it would erase her soul.

Kazjivo dashed forward, straight into the

pointed edge of Arcus' blade. The white energy beam smashed into him, blasting him backwards.

At least I was able to see her one last time.

–

"Comrade, to think you would sacrifice your life, for good this time, for the villainous lady..." remarked Arcus. He stood over Kazjivo's limp body, waiting for his soul to appear.

This charge had everything put into it. It wasn't a charge done in haste. It wasn't a half charge that was interrupted mid-swing. No, this was Arcus' full power blast wave. It was strong enough to destroy star systems. Kazjivo stood no chance. To think, the fool would've been able to kill Arcus, had he dodged it, let Villin die, then kill Arcus himself. But he had to save his wife.

Fool.

He was still led on by his emotions. She'd tricked him into marrying her. How did he fall for her, even after knowing the truth? Was he that desperate? That lonely? That *defective?*

None of that mattered now, however. He'd had to kill Villin before Kazjivo's soul arrived. Technique machines didn't completely die when killed. Their soul would remain in the higher dimension, alive.

There was one way to get it back—by taking the life of another higher-dimensional being.

Those nightmares of Hardt's weren't dreams. He was actually in the higher dimension, being slowly lured towards Arcus. And when he got close enough, Arcus took his life. Twice. Once your soul died in the higher dimension, you died forever. Arcus took the remnants of Hardt's soul and reappeared in Hardt's room, alive. Breathing. In the world of the living, the third dimension.

He had taken Hardt's phone, cracked the pin, then messaged Villin, hoping she'd fall for the bait. Oh, she did. She really went to Einel alone. And so, she died.

Now aware of her assailant, however, she ran away from him. Dodged his every attack. Ran like the coward she was, abusing her Technique, moving at lightning speed. It would take a long charge to take her out. It'd need to be absolutely massive, so massive she wouldn't be able to run out in time. So he broke the rear blade off his greatsword. Charging the greatsword with his right hand, blasting her with the broken blade of the other, keeping her away from him.

Arcus paused, mid-internal monologue. It had been a while now and Kazjivo's soul wasn't coming out. Did he not have one? Well, his body wasn't disappearing... huh.

Arcus walked up to Kazjivo's body, peering intensely. Grey, wispy smoke was around him, seeping slowly into his body.

The... hell?

He recalled the past, when he had dragged Kazjivo's body back to his ship. It had the same grey glow then, a thin veil of mist, ever so slowly seeping in.

Was he... still alive?

No, that couldn't be possible. The blast wave was his ultimate attack, depleting most of his energy. It would've destroyed a literal star system, half a light-year across. But here Kazjivo lay, listless, but existing.

Arcus raised his single-bladed greatsword, preparing to stab downwards and finish the job. It would probably take the rest of his Technique to finish him off. He'd have to worry about that Technique-control abusing coward Villin later.

Wait.

Villin.

The golden flash appeared for only the briefest of moments before he felt the blade pierce his chest. The blade came from a kilometer away, its length stretching just as long.

As he was lifted into space, he could feel

himself dying. His blue blood dripped onto the long nodachi, staining it briefly before it turned to dust.

The blade retracted, carrying him towards the owner of the weapon. Once close enough, he could see who it was,

She wore all black; she had a gunmetal grey metal arm, had golden hair which flowed to her waist. Villin.

The nodachi finally returned to its regular size, leaving Arcus only a meter away from her. Villin kicked Arcus off the blade; as he fell off, his body faded away, turning into dust.

A glittering white light appeared; it hovered in place, beaming its dazzling glow nearby. Villin approached it, her normal hand outstretched. Once her hand made contact with it, the light flashed impossibly bright, causing her to flinch. When she opened her eyes, she could feel something had changed within her.

She was alive.

–

The song was beautiful. One I'd heard a million times. Villin had often sung it around the ship, and I'd listen, entranced by the addicting melody. Then, it stopped.

"Ahem. Day ninety-two, 12:00 hours. My darling remains in a coma. The grey glow emanates from him, as usual. Donated a trillion to help fix Bastea. People are starting to wonder where Kazjivo is. They haven't seen him with me for a while now. Not sure how much longer I can avoid answering the press. Signing out."

I slowly opened my eyes; there she sat, writing in a logbook. About me, I suppose. She was waiting for me to come back.

I must've made a noise when I turned, for she suddenly whipped her head around, staring at me. She quickly rushed over, cradling my face.

"K-Kaz... do you remember me?"

Tears had started to form in her pretty, violetish-blue eyes, as she spoke, staring at me intently. It entranced me.

Chug...

Chug...

Chug...

The ship's engines were vibrating softly in the distance.

Just like when we first met.

—

Villin lowered her head onto the bed, sobbing. Kazjivo had a blank stare on his face, as if he didn't know her. This time, she really knew him. This time, she really was his wife. But all those memories would be gone. It hurt. It hurt bad.

Suddenly, she felt a familiar hand lace through her golden hair, caressing her. She turned her head, slowly, in disbelief; it was Kazjivo, and he was looking at her with that loving gaze in his eyes.

"Of course I remember you, Villin."

She shrieked in joy, then kissed him, giving

him a hug he couldn't get out of (to be fair, he was still injured). She wouldn't let go. Not now, not ever. Her Kazjivo was back.

As he returned her embrace, he thought of the memories he created and shared with her. She was always there for him, guiding him through life. The beautiful lies she had carefully crafted for him. Her confidence and bravery. Her curtness towards others, indifference for humans. Those traits made her uniquely her. Uniquely Villin.

And she is perfect just the way she is.

T H E   E N D

STAR SYSTEMS

— — — —

The Galactic Alliance of Milky Way

Star: Cosmo | Planet: Radi | Capital | Radii

Star: Dos | Planet: Trojan | Capital: Tamki | City: Dlli

Star: Klarodon | Planet: Wentsival | Capital: Achent

Star: Kotqoyusal | Planet: Miutkyli | Capital: Utyski

Stars: Kyan, Jyan | Planet: KJ4 | Capital: 0016

Star: Lua | Planets: Eviel, Einel (D) | Capital: Argua

Star: Mallent | Planet: Malwer | Capital: Maker

Star: Mscrhmer | Planet: Ranktel | Capital: Nordt

Star: Pegasi | Planet: Ers | Capital: Vont

Star: Sol | Planets: Earth, Mars, Nades | Capitals:
Bastea, Olympus, Naberus

Star: Tau | Planets: Ceti, Volke | Capitals: Taurus, Eve

Stars: Tor, Core, Pyro | Planet: Argona | Capital: Vomra

TECHNIQUE MACHINES

– – – –

	CODE	POWER	TECH.	COMP.	HUMANITY
KAZJIVO KUBA	X-07	10	10	10	1
HARDT BREIKR	13H	7	5	10	10
ARCUS AYTFRI	83A	10	9	8	5
MIKALEV SCHREN	700M	9	8	7	8
VILLIN DEVILLE	925k Da	8	10	9	5

Power: Max power draw from the higher dimension.

Technique: Ability to manipulate the higher dimension.

Compute: Computational/network power.

Humanity: 'Human' score as decided by Dr. Khamv.

ARGUA

- - - -

Villin's modded spaceship (Argua)

A small to medium-sized ship, it has a large back
chassis that can house people and controls. The engines
are separated from the main chassis, leading outwards
from the bottom, then forwards. Each of these sections
house a giant engine. The engine section housing is
angular and looks like a giant X from the front. The
housing looks like a large rectangular prism, with a 90-
degree triangle at the front end. There are some rudders
behind the engines and upwards, connected to the main
chassis. They are also X shaped when viewed from the
front. Mounted on the main chassis and both engine
housings are ten giant railguns for space combat. Two
are on the main chassis; two on each side of the pilot's
windows. Two are on each engine housing, stacked
vertically.

TRIVIA

— — — —

- The dwarf planet Arcus had lured his victims to is Einel from Lua star system.

- Arcus ended up killing eighteen billion people.

- Mikalev Schren was named after... Dr. Schren.

- The first letter of each machine spell out a certain doctor.

- Villin has $92,500,000,000 in her bank.

- The girl Mikalev searches for is Rudy.

- Once you finish the book, re-read *Splitting Paths;* see if you can figure out how many years pass between scene 2 to 3.

- Kazjivo's POV journal is from *Who am I?* to *Diary.*

- The twelfth council member (of Lua), has less power than other members. Represented by a surviving citizen of Eviel.

Author's note

————

"No Fenne" has never written a book before.
Here is your reward for finishing my first novel.

Concept Art - 925

www.ingramcontent.com/pod-product-compliance
Lightning Source LLC
Chambersburg PA
CBHW030409180626
46812CB00005B/1981